hot springs murder

Alaska Cozy Mystery - 8

wendy meadows

Wendy Meadows

Majestic Owl Publishing LLC

This is a work of fiction. Names, characters, places, and incidents are a product of the author's imagination. Locales and public names are sometimes used for atmospheric purposes. Any resemblance to actual people, living or dead, or to businesses, companies, events, institutions, or locales is completely coincidental.

Majestic Owl Publishing LLC
P.O. Box 997
Newport, NH 03773

Created with Vellum

chapter one

"Smell that?" asked Conrad, pushing Sarah's soft hair away from her eyes as they stood together on the front porch. He motioned toward the rugged, lush landscape of Alaska surrounding the cabin they both now called home. "Winter is coming."

Sarah looked around and studied her cabin and the land. Her cabin sat nestled up against the land like a fragile child being hugged by a dangerous yet unimaginable beauty. The early morning air was slowly turning colder and colder, filling with the scent of an early snow. The sunrise sky was a reddish-pink, mixed with a few gray clouds pushing over the blue. The breath was leaving her mouth in weak trails which would soon become thick white paths. Yes, winter was approaching and very quickly at that. Sarah felt grateful to be wearing the thick green wool sweater that was keeping her warm. "I'm looking forward to the snow," she smiled.

Conrad nodded and burrowed into the collar of his black leather jacket. "I like the snow, too," he told Sarah and gently kissed her forehead. "I better get down to the station before Andrew drinks up all the coffee. Also, the new deputy is coming today, and I want to be around when he arrives."

Conrad pulled open the driver's side door to his truck. "Are you going to O'Mally's with Amanda?"

"Girls day out," Sarah told Conrad in an excited voice. "Amanda and I are going to shop until we drop." Sarah reached into the truck and grabbed the seatbelt. "We'll probably have lunch at the diner after and spend the rest of the day at the coffee shop. Since I finished the book, I have time to devote to the coffee shop."

Conrad took the seatbelt from Sarah and buckled up. "I'll meet you there after my shift," he promised.

"We can have dinner at the diner," Sarah smiled. "Besides, I'm going to need a strong man to carry home all my shopping bags." Sarah touched Conrad's nose. "You be careful."

"Sarah, Snow Falls has been very, very quiet," Conrad pointed out. "I think we're really past the storm."

"Still," Sarah said in a careful voice, "let's not take the quiet for granted. There is still a world full of dangerous people out there, Conrad. We may be enjoying peace here in Snow Falls, but that peace can be shattered at any second by the real world."

"Yeah, that's true enough," Conrad agreed. He looked at Sarah's beautiful face and nodded his head. "I'll be careful. I promise."

Sarah smiled. "I know you will," she said, "and I'll be careful, too. All I want to do today is go shopping with Amanda, tinker around in my coffee shop, have dinner at the diner, and then come home and cuddle up to a good book while you watch your game show."

"Sounds like a good day to me," Conrad agreed. He closed the driver's door, rolled down the window, and nodded his head toward the cabin. "You better walk Mittens before she messes up the kitchen floor."

"Good idea," Sarah replied. She stepped back from Conrad's truck and waved goodbye as he backed down the drive and drove away. "Please be careful," she whispered and hurried back into the kitchen. Mittens was waiting at the back door, with a look of disappointment on her face. "I know, honey, I know," Sarah apologized. She quickly hooked Mittens to a gray leash and walked her outside. Mittens made her way to the backyard, sniffed the air, and looked around. Finding a good spot to use the bathroom, she watered the land. "Good girl," Sarah told Mittens in a pleased voice as a truck pulled into her driveway. "That will be Amanda."

Sarah walked Mittens to the front of the cabin and waved at Amanda. "Good morning."

Amanda waved back with an excited hand and burst out of her truck like a woman who had just received a million-dollar check. "Los Angeles!" she yelled in a happy voice. Amanda ran up to Sarah, patted Mittens on her head, and then fished a piece of paper out of the right pocket of a deep blue coat. "Look at this," she beamed.

Sarah made a curious face. She handed Amanda the leash, took the piece of paper, and read it. "Snow Creek Hot Spring Resort?" she asked.

"You bet, love," Amanda beamed.

"I don't understand?" Sarah asked, and lowered the paper. She looked at Amanda with confused eyes.

"You will," Amanda promised. She grabbed Sarah's right hand and dragged her inside to the kitchen. "Go lay down, girl," she told Mittens and unhooked the husky from her leash. Mittens licked Amanda's hand, walked to the far right corner of the kitchen, and laid down on a soft brown doggy bed.

"Coffee?" Sarah asked, as she closed the back door. The kitchen was warm and smelled of coffee and pancakes. Sarah took a second to enjoy the atmosphere and smell, replaying the cozy breakfast she had shared with her husband over in her mind, before pouring two fresh cups of coffee.

"Thank you," Amanda said, taking a brown mug of coffee

from Sarah and hurrying to the kitchen table. She sat down and studied a plate full of fresh cinnamon rolls. Grabbing one, she took a very deep breath full of nervous excitement. "Love, you know I love you."

Sarah cautiously sat down at the kitchen table and studied her best friend with alert eyes. "Uh oh," she said in a worried voice as her mind suddenly understood just what the 'Snow Creek Hot Springs Resort' was.

"Now, don't throw me off a cliff before you hear me out," Amanda pleaded. She took a bite of her cinnamon roll and washed it down with a sip of coffee. "Snow Creek Hot Springs Resort is a diamond in the rough."

"Honey, when you said you were thinking of starting your own business, I thought of a dress shop or a bakery."

"So did I," Amanda said, in an excited voice. "But," she said, as she quickly polished off her cinnamon roll, "when my dear hubby and I visited the hot springs last week I changed my mind. Oh, I feel like I'm in love. And to my shock, the resort is for sale!"

"Amanda, honey, the resort is also a two-hour drive north of us," Sarah pointed out. "All alone—in the middle of nowhere."

"I know," Amanda nearly burst, "isn't it great? The remote location of the resort is absolutely darling." Amanda took a sip of her coffee. "One road in, one road out."

"A very dangerous, winding, mountain road as I recall," Sarah added. "If you get caught up there in the winter, you're snow-shoeing home."

"That's why we'll only be open when the road is passable."

"We?" Sarah asked and gulped. "June Bug, honey, I can't—"

"You said you would help me run my business," Amanda reminded Sarah in a pleading voice. "You promised," she said, and made a very sad face.

"I know I promised, honey, but… a resort… in the middle of nowhere?" Sarah quickly sipped at her coffee. "I—"

"You just finished your new book," Amanda quickly cut Sarah off at the pass. She had to act fast and throw a net over her best friend. "There hasn't been any trouble in months, and we've been on our best behavior."

"I know, honey, but—"

Amanda stepped on the accelerator. "You promised to help me," she pointed out for the second time and made another sad face. "You said you would be my business partner, love. I thought... we were... sisters."

"We are sisters," Sarah promised.

"Through thick and thin?"

"Of course," Sarah assured Amanda.

Amanda's face tossed off the sadness and jumped into a pool of joy. "Good, then you'll go into business with me. I'm sure going to need all the help I can get now that my dear hubby has once again flown back to London." Amanda stopped smiling and looked down at her coffee. "I need this, Los Angeles. I don't like it when my husband leaves me alone. I know he's doing what he thinks is right, but I worry about him so. I need something to take my mind off my troubles."

"Is buying a resort the answer?" Sarah asked.

Amanda nodded her head. "The resort is very small, with just a few private cabins, four to be exact. There is the main lodge, of course, and the hot springs area is located behind the resort down a long trail. It's not like I'm buying a resort on some tropical island that pulls in a million people a year. I mean, blimey, my husband and I were the only guests at the resort when we visited." Amanda looked up at Sarah. "I want to buy this resort, Los Angeles. Because I want something to call my own, you know? And to share with those I love."

Sarah studied the eyes of her best friend. She saw a desperate woman who, for whatever reason, had her heart set on the idea of buying a remote resort that sat out in the middle of nowhere. "Winter is approaching very quickly," she pointed out.

"I know," Amanda nodded, and allowed excitement to reclaim her voice. "I figured we could take a trip to the resort next Monday once all the paperwork is signed. We'd spend a week getting the place ready for winter, then go back when the snow melts."

Sarah took a sip of coffee. The idea of helping her friend prepare her new business for winter didn't seem too unreasonable. After all, Sarah reminded herself, she did promise Amanda help in whatever business endeavor her friend chose to begin. Besides, winter was rapidly approaching, and what harm could there be in tying down a few cabins before the snow arrived? "Honey, who are you buying the resort from?" she asked, easing off her objections.

"Mr. Colt Grayman," Amanda said, in a proud voice.

"Who is Colt Grayman?"

"Well, my dear and not so subtle detective friend, Mr. Grayman is a seventy-four-year-old bloke who looks like a dried-up prune and talks like one, too. He built the resort in 1978 with his wife and has finally decided to move the poor old woman to Florida where it's nice and warm," Amanda explained. "Mr. Grayman is not a man of many words, but I got enough out of him to know he's a decent fellow who is tired of hard winters."

"Keep talking."

Amanda took a sip of coffee. "I managed to talk Mr. Grayman into selling me the resort under his asking price. Several thousand dollars under his asking price, to be exact."

Sarah studied Amanda's eyes. "Your dear hubby has no idea you're buying this resort, does he? If he did, you would be opening a dress shop. You went behind his back, didn't you? And you unleashed your charm on a defenseless old man."

Amanda bit down on her lower lip and made a pained face. "I wanted it to be a surprise," she gulped. "When my hubby returns from London and the snow melts away, we'll go back to the resort and I'll surprise him. He really loved the resort when we were there."

"Did he?" Sarah asked, and grinned at Amanda.

"Well," Amanda confessed and made another pained face, "he especially liked the hot springs."

Sarah laughed. "You're a mess," she told Amanda in a loving voice.

"I know," Amanda admitted. "I guess I should have told him, but he might have said no. Besides, I deserve to buy something I truly want. I've earned it, after all."

"Yes, you have, June Bug," Sarah agreed. She reached across the table and patted Amanda's hand. "I'll help you prepare your resort for the winter—but you have to handle your husband alone."

"Oh, thank you!" Amanda yelled. She jumped to her feet, ran to Sarah, and hugged her. "We're going to make our resort into something great, just wait and see. We'll turn those stuffy old cabins into something romantic and fun. I envision charming and quaint, cozy and inviting. We'll spruce up the trail leading to the hot springs and maybe even add a few benches. We'll—"

"Let's focus on the here and now," Sarah laughed. "First, we need to focus on actually buying the resort."

"I called Mr. Grayman. He's going to meet me Monday at the resort with his attorney. His wife has already left for Florida. As soon as I sign the papers and hand him the check, he's driving to Anchorage and taking the first flight to Florida." Amanda let go of Sarah. "The resort is basically in good shape, minus a few bumps and bruises from some very hard winters. All we need to do is spend a week tying the place down for winter, then come home, wait out the snow, and when the flowers bloom, go back and get to work!"

Sarah looked up into Amanda's excited and terrified face. Her best friend was beginning a new chapter in her life that was filled with uncertain adventure. How could she say no? "I'll bring the bleach."

"You bet!" Amanda clapped her hands and sat back down. She took another cinnamon roll and let out a deep breath. "I can see it now, Los Angeles, we're going to make a splash! We're going to turn an unknown hot springs resort into something special… and really put it on the map. Who knows, maybe we'll build more cabins... add a restaurant... a dance hall... everything." Amanda's eyes shone as she continued working over the cinnamon rolls. "We're going to make a proper go at this."

Sarah reached out and took a cinnamon roll. "You're paying for the gas," she joked. "And you're the one who's going to have to convince Conrad to let me go. After our last case Conrad doesn't like me leaving his sight that much."

"Can you blame him?" Amanda asked. "You were attacked by a madman and we were all nearly killed. I can't fault Conrad for worrying."

"It's been peaceful since our last case," Sarah told Amanda. "I truly think the storm is over. We've dealt with some pretty harsh foes and come out into the sunshine."

"Yeah, that's true," Amanda agreed. "My dear hubby felt that it was safe enough to leave me alone again." Amanda tossed a thumb at the back door. "I don't walk around town looking over my shoulder half as much as I used to, either."

Sarah nodded her head. "I know just what you mean," she said, and took a sip of coffee. She grew silent and let her mind think. "We'll be traveling two hours north to a very remote location. I doubt we'll encounter a gang of killers out there."

"Maybe a grumpy bear or two," Amanda joked. "Or maybe a skunk taking a dip in the hot springs."

Sarah smiled. "If we find a skunk taking a midnight dip, I'm going to run straight home."

Amanda clapped her hands. "Oh, this is going to be so much fun. Just think—little ol' me owning a resort. Why I could just cry."

"Don't cry until after you've convinced Conrad to let me go," Sarah laughed, and stood up. "In the meantime, we have some shopping to do."

"Yes, we do!" Amanda cheered and prepared for a great day.

Sarah's jeep crawled up the narrow dirt road surrounded by rugged mountain land. She had come to adore the Alaskan wilderness, with its untamed voice that man would never be able to harm. The wilderness made her feel free; free from the loud, crowded world of Los Angeles she'd once called home, where society was spoiled with large cities and people were unwilling to even venture into the forest, much less the wild landscape of Alaska. Alongside her admiration, though, was a respect for the dangers the wilderness presented—including the road she was currently navigating. "My goodness," she said, the engine revving as the vehicle crawled over a deep bump, "this isn't a road, Amanda, it is more like a goat trail!"

Amanda, holding on for dear life, quickly rolled down her window and stuck her head out. Crisp, cool, fresh air struck her face. The air was meandering through tall, winter-worn trees that reached up toward a powerful mountain that had yet to be scarred by the footprint of man. All she saw was miles and miles of wilderness stretching out forever—or so it seemed. Through a group of trees, she spotted the shimmering waters of Snow Ice Lake—a small lake that Mr. Grayman had told her about, which was very difficult to reach but full of delicious fish. "There's the lake—I think—so we have about a mile or so left," she told Sarah in a quick voice.

"Thank goodness," Sarah sighed, as her jeep moved forward and maneuvered over a deep rut. She was wearing a brown long-sleeved dress and felt very hot, even though the air was cool. Amanda, on the other hand, was wrapped up in a heavy blue coat and brown boots, ready for war—or so it seemed. "June Bug, this road is going to need some work."

"I know, I know." Amanda sighed and pulled her head back into the jeep. "My dear hubby complained about this road more times than I care to relate. But," Amanda said in a determined voice, "one step at a time. We'll go meet Mr. Grayman, hand him the check, and get to work preparing our resort for the winter."

"Our?" Sarah asked.

"Yes," Amanda smiled. "Los Angeles, I consider your coffee shop yours and mine. I want the resort to be the same. I want us to share everything. Besides, if my dear hubby thinks you're my business partner, I'll have a better chance at maintaining ownership of the resort when he returns home from London!"

Sarah grinned, "I am but a pawn on your chessboard of life."

"You sure are, love." Amanda grinned back and patted Sarah's arm. "Now, keep driving very slowly and keep your eyes on the road."

"Path," Sarah mumbled under her breath.

"I heard that," Amanda said, and nudged Sarah with her elbow.

Sarah began to reply but slammed on the brakes instead. The jeep jerked and came to a hard stop just as a large grizzly bear wandered out onto the road. "Oh my!" Sarah whispered as the color drained from her face.

"Don't move," Amanda whimpered and grabbed Sarah's arm.

Sarah debated on whether to back her jeep away from the bear, but she knew she wouldn't get far. The jeep could only move forward at no more than ten miles an hour. Backing down the road would be far slower, at a speed a large grizzly bear could easily catch. "We're like fish in a barrel," she whispered to Amanda as the big bear stood in the middle of the road just staring at the jeep.

"I didn't need to hear that," Amanda whimpered again. She kept her eyes locked on the bear and began to pray.

The grizzly, who appeared bored and sleepy, suddenly sat down on his backside and simply looked at the jeep. "No," Sarah begged, "don't sit down. Shoo! Get out of the way," she pleaded and made moving motions with her hands. "Go that way... off into the woods." The grizzly bear reached up a powerful paw and swatted at his nose, then went back to staring at the jeep.

"We're food," Amanda said in a pained voice.

Amanda's words caused an idea to race into Sarah's mind. Sarah quickly turned in her seat, reached around, and grabbed a small green cooler. "Food," she said, and carefully opened the cooler. "Peanut butter and jelly sandwiches, to be exact."

"Los Angeles? Love...what are you doing?" Amanda asked, in a dread-filled voice.

Sarah slowly grabbed four sandwiches out of the cooler, removed each sandwich from its sandwich bag, reached her left hand out of the driver's window, and began throwing each sandwich toward the rear of the jeep. "Food! Come and eat, big fella!" she yelled.

"Oh my," Amanda gasped, and quickly rolled up the passenger window.

Sarah pulled her left arm back into the jeep, rolled up the window, and waited for the grizzly bear to act. To her relief, the bear began sniffing the air, looked toward the jeep with curious eyes, and then stood up. "Take the food," Sarah begged.

The grizzly slowly began to lumber toward the jeep.

"Here he comes," Amanda whimpered and threw her hands over her face, waiting for the jeep to slashed open by its claws. To her shock—and relief—the bear walked past the driver's side door, made his way to the back of the jeep, and then began searching for the sandwiches. Sarah didn't wait. She carefully pressed down on the gas pedal and got the jeep moving, leaving the bear safely behind eating a mid-morning snack. Amanda turned in her seat, spotted the bear eating a sandwich, and let out a heavy breath. "Los Angeles, you are my hero."

"A hero with shaky hands," Sarah confessed, and then let out a nervous laugh. "That was a very large grizzly bear."

"He could have cut this jeep in two with just one paw," Amanda agreed and looked at Sarah. "We won't tell our hubbies about the bear, okay?"

"Deal," Sarah agreed and looked into the outside mirror. She spotted the grizzly bear eating a second sandwich. "I don't think that big fellow is going to chase us."

Amanda wiped at her forehead. "We are in the middle of nowhere," she explained. "Mr. Grayman did warn me this land belongs to the animals and not man."

"Are you having second thoughts?" Sarah asked, easing around a bend which pushed the jeep out of the bear's line of sight.

"Oh no," Amanda replied, in a tough voice. "No bear is going to scare me away from achieving my dream." Amanda glanced over her shoulder toward the bend. "I've seen bears in Snow Falls. That doesn't mean I'm not going to step outside my home."

Sarah looked at Amanda and then smiled. She felt proud of her best friend. "Well then," she said, "we better make up for the time we lost back there. It's almost time to meet Mr. Grayman."

"I called Mr. Grayman from the telephone at that old gas station we stopped at," Amanda told Sarah. "While you were filling the jeep with gas, I also sneaked in a few candy bars." Amanda patted her coat pockets.

Sarah rolled her eyes. "Why am I not surprised, June Bug?" she asked.

Amanda grinned. "Never take me for granted, Los Angeles," she replied and continued. "Anyway, Mr. Grayman said he has his plane ticket in hand. All he's waiting for is me to get there and sign on the dotted line."

"His attorney is here, right?" Sarah asked, in a hopeful voice. "June Bug, this sale has to be legal in every single aspect. You're going to need legal papers to secure the transfer of—"

"Mr. Grayman assured me that Mr. Fields is on the property," Amanda assured Sarah.

"Good," Sarah told her best friend as she carefully moved over a thick root climbing across the road. They bounced in their seats as the vehicle's shocks jolted across it. "My jeep is taking a beating."

"I'll work on the road later," Amanda promised. "Right now, all I want to do is sign on the dotted line, wave goodbye to Mr. Grayman, and get to work." Amanda rolled down the passenger's side window and let fresh, cool air into the jeep. "Oh, June Bug, the resort is so cozy. The cabins are simply charming, and the main lodge is a place a person could snuggle up in all winter—well, it will be when we're finished." Amanda let her eyes fall out across the rugged landscape. "I guess calling our new business a resort isn't so wise," she spoke after a minute.

"Well, we're not really going to a resort, are we?" Sarah asked. "More like a—mountain hideaway."

Amanda bit down on her lip. "Maybe we should name our business—" Amanda rubbed her cheek, "maybe—Snow Creek Hideaway and Springs?"

"How about Snow Creek Springs?" Sarah suggested. "The name is simple, remains original, but takes off the false gold."

"Snow Creek Springs—I like it!" Amanda beamed and patted Sarah's arm, "Thanks, Los Angeles."

Sarah smiled, "How much further, honey?"

"A mile, I guess," Amanda replied. "See how the road is starting to climb? That means we're very close to the re—I mean, to our hideaway," Amanda said, using a secretive voice full of playful humor.

Sarah looked to her left and soaked in the view of the land. "June Bug, this really is a hideaway," she pointed out. "We're miles from the nearest town—miles from any hospital, police station, or gas station. If someone were to get hurt, a medical helicopter would have to fly in here. We're not talking about a little clubhouse behind your parents' house. We're traveling deeper and deeper north, straight into wild, untamed wilderness."

"I understand the dangers," Amanda told Sarah in a calm voice.

"I know you do, honey," Sarah nodded her head. "I know you understand the dangers more than anyone else. You're not the type of woman to rush into a decision without investigating every single corner of the room first. I'm sure you have every cautious concern placed in a binder, stored and studied."

Amanda reached into the right pocket of her coat and pulled out a caramel candy bar wrapped in a green and gold wrapper. "I've spent the last few days going over every single detail," she confessed. "I've considered the dangers—the pros and the cons—the ups and downs." Amanda opened her candy bar. "There is one phone on the property," she continued. "About twenty years ago, an old research station stood where the main lodge stands now. The state managed to run an underground phone wire all the way to the station. The station was privately funded, and someone paid some big bucks to have the phone line run from the station down to the main road."

Sarah listened to Amanda talk. "I bet," she said.

Amanda nodded her head and continued, stepping away from the topic of an old research station that had been closed down and forgotten about. "There is a clearing for a helicopter to land if injury occurs," she told Sarah. "It's about a quarter of a mile east of the main lodge. The trail leading to the hot springs is well marked and easily navigable." Amanda munched on her candy bar. "There are some heavy duty generators sitting in the sheds that are off to the back of the cabins and lodge. The generators are solar powered, which is really neat—but costly. Mr. Grayman added in the cost of each generator to his selling price. He knocked a couple thousand dollars off because the generators are used and not new."

"Solar generators are good to have."

"Sure beats hauling gas up here all the time," Amanda agreed. She polished off her candy bar. "Los Angeles, I've dotted my 'i's, and crossed all my 't's."

"I know, honey."

"And it's not like we're going to be entertaining hundreds of guests," Amanda said, and looked out of her window. "Mr. Grayman said my dear hubby and I were the third couple he's had in over a month. People will come—but in tiny trickles. And that's okay. I don't want to buy a resort and build miles of parking lots. I want a quiet, cozy place that brings in a handful of guests a month."

"You want to hide away from the world," Sarah told Amanda and quickly bit her lip. "Oh honey, I'm sorry."

"No, no, it's true," Amanda confessed. "After all we've been through, Los Angeles; after all the crazies we've fought. Like the Back Alley Killer, that insane model building those creepy snowmen, Mr. Mafia, that mental FBI agent, Ms. Bad Daughter, and that troubled kid in Oregon," Amanda sighed. "It's true. I do want to hide away from the world, in a place that is my own—our own—but a place that can still have life to it." Amanda looked at Sarah with desperate eyes. "Does that make any sense, love? Probably not."

"Makes perfect sense," Sarah smiled. "Conrad and I bought that remote cabin, remember? We take hikes back to the cabin when we can. That's our place to hide away from the world."

Amanda folded her arms and smiled. "I want this place, Los Angeles. I can't explain it—but in my heart, this place is calling out to me. I feel excited and scared, anxious and uncertain—but so hopeful. Oh, so very hopeful. For the first time in my life, I'm stepping outside of my own safe zone, not because I'm forced to, but because I want to." Amanda let out a tired laugh. "I would rather face a grizzly bear than the creeps we've had to face in the past."

Sarah laughed. "I second that," she agreed, and looked at her best friend. "We'll turn your place into a charming getaway in the woods," she promised. "Come spring, we'll force our husbands to haul everything we need up here and get to work."

Amanda smiled. "I'm glad you said that because I've drawn some designs for the main lodge. I'm thinking of keeping the atmosphere rustic, yet I want a vintage look, which means we have some antique shopping to do."

Sarah's eyes lit up as she said, "I love to go antiquing."

"Me, too," Amanda giggled as Sarah brought the jeep around another bend in the road. When the jeep cleared the bend, the road began a steeper climb. After what seemed like forever, the road came to an end at a dirt parking lot designed to accommodate no more than four vehicles. A hiking trail led away from the parking lot and zoomed north. "End of the road," Sarah announced, and parked next to a rough, weather-torn gray truck.

"Just the beginning, actually," Amanda promised, and looked at the trail leading to the main lodge. As she did, a strange feeling swept through her heart—a bad feeling.

Something was wrong—horribly wrong. She didn't remember the lodge being so far from the parking lot, for one thing. "I—guess we better get our hiking shoes on," she said, and forced a nervous smile to her lips, afraid to confess her feeling to Sarah.

chapter two

Sarah grabbed a heavy brown backpack and, using every ounce of energy she had, hoisted it onto her back. "Ready?" she asked, looking around. The last thing Sarah wanted was to spot the grizzly bear she had encountered down the road. She glanced down at the brown hiking boots she was wearing and hoped they'd be light enough to lend her some speed if the bear appeared on the trail.

"Almost," Amanda said, placing a green pack over her shoulders and grabbing the small food cooler. "We can come back for the blankets and cleaning supplies later."

Sarah nodded her head. "I want to get acquainted with my surroundings before we start preparing this place for the winter," she explained. "I would like to spend the day walking around and doing a little exploring—if that's okay with you, June Bug."

"That'll be fine," Amanda assured Sarah and cast her eyes at the trail leading to the main lodge. Her stomach filled with worry and dread.

Sarah spotted the sudden cloud in Amanda's eyes. She closed the driver's side door to the jeep and walked over to her best friend. "June Bug, honey, what's the matter?"

"Huh?" Amanda asked, in a distant voice. She slowly turned her head and locked eyes with Sarah. "Why would anything be the matter?"

Sarah turned her head and studied the trail. "Because you're looking at that trail like it's going to lead you into a grave," she pointed out.

"Don't be silly," Amanda replied and closed the passenger's door. "After all, this trip was all my idea, right?"

"Yes," Sarah agreed. "But, June Bug, we can always turn around and drive home. You haven't signed any papers and, as of now, you're simply a guest. You have no obligation to continue on this venture if you're starting to feel uncomfortable."

Amanda glanced around. The landscape was absolutely breathtaking. She raised her eyes and studied a mountain that stood with strength and mystery. The top of the mountain was already showing white. "Look around, Los Angeles—this land is beautiful. And listen—what do you hear?"

Sarah listened. "The wind, and birds."

"Exactly," Amanda pointed out. She focused back on the trail. "Do you realize that maybe twenty people at the most travel this road during the course of a year? That's what Mr. Grayman told me. No more than twenty people. Most of those people travel in a single vehicle like we did. This place is untouched—pure." Amanda kept her eyes on the trail. "When I left London, I was very heartbroken. After all, I'm a city girl, right?"

"Right," Sarah agreed.

"I grew up walking on sidewalks. The only wilderness I knew was taking holidays to the countryside and visiting my Aunt Rachel," Amanda continued. "I never knew such places like this even existed." Amanda finally looked at Sarah. "Honey, I'm growing older—we both are. Sure, we're not old biddies—not yet—but we're a long way from eighteen. It's time for me to have a place to call my own. My hubby picked out our cabin—he chose Snow Falls." Amanda took her eyes back to the trail. "All I'm trying to say is that I need something that the world hasn't polluted—something I found all on my own."

Sarah focused on the trail. "We're really far out," she reminded Amanda. "I don't think the world has touched this beautiful piece of the world." Sarah smiled tentatively. "Ready?"

Amanda drew in a deep breath. "I'm ready," she said, even though her gut whispered at her to run. Something just wasn't right. A darkness had invaded her special hideaway. Amanda felt it inside her heart. But she told herself this was just a bad case of the jitters, a little nervousness as she embarked on a big adventure. After all, she was a little nervous about not telling her husband in advance about all this. Perhaps it was nothing more than that. So instead of telling Sarah, she marched to the trail and pointed up a hill. "The trail goes up a steep hill, levels off and then goes for about a quarter of a mile and ends up at the main lodge."

Sarah studied the trail and then glanced back at the parking lot. "I hope Mr. Grayman drove his attorney up here from the main road," she pointed out, "because my jeep and that truck are the only two vehicles in sight."

Amanda had noticed a third vehicle wasn't present and didn't say anything. She knew Sarah, being a former homicide detective from Los Angeles—a woman who had worked deadly streets and chased down ruthless killers—would notice that a third vehicle was missing. The fact of the matter was that the missing vehicle was indeed worrying Sarah. "Let's hope," she said, and began walking up the steep hill, stepping over broken sticks and rocks.

"Let's hope," Sarah whispered back and followed Amanda, feeling the weight of her gun pressing against her right ankle. She knew her gun was no match for a grizzly bear —but a human would surely take a bullet and stay down.

Amanda glanced over her shoulder, tossed a weak smile at Sarah, and focused back on the trail as her mind grew silent and still. She didn't say a word until the trail ended and came up behind a large log cabin with a cozy wraparound porch attached to it. The cabin acted as the main lodge, standing in a wide clearing filled with wildflowers and grass that had never been touched by the blade of a lawnmower. Four smaller cabins sat side by side next to the large one, like obedient children waiting for a treat. Each cabin faced north toward an open field with a large, powerful river running through it. Beyond the field stood the mountain—majestic and breathtaking. The mountain looked down on the rugged scene with loving eyes, overlooking the five cabins standing in a small clearing surrounded by wild land. "Here we are," Amanda announced in a careful voice. She stopped walking and studied the back of the main cabin and began searching for signs of where Mr. Grayman might be.

Sarah walked up to Amanda and looked across the land. "Gosh, it's beautiful," she said, catching her breath. "Now I can see why you wanted to buy this place so badly. I don't think I've ever seen land so beautiful in my life. And look over there—a river—and look at that mountain! The scenery alone is enough to make a person melt."

"It is beautiful," Amanda agreed. For a mere second, she managed to push the storm in her heart away and focus on the beauty of the land. "I would love to explore that mountain," she told Sarah. "I would love to get a boat and travel that river—have a picnic—so many wonderful things." Amanda looked toward the river. "I would love for my hubby to take me for a romantic walk. I don't think that's asking for too much, do you?"

"Not at all," Sarah told Amanda, and rubbed her friend's shoulder with her hand. "Someday soon," she promised. "Now, we better go find Mr. Grayman."

"I suppose we should," Amanda agreed. She turned and

focused back on the land and maneuvered around to the front of the cabin, unaware that two deadly eyes were watching her every step from behind a large tree in the distance.

"Mr. Grayman?" Amanda called out as she reached the front of the cabin. An old-fashioned hand pump well stood in front of the cabin, surrounded by a wooden flower box full of weeds instead of flowers. It was clear to anyone with any common sense that the owners of the resort had given up on it long ago. "Mr. Grayman?"

Sarah stepped up to the front of the cabin and studied the set of wooden steps leading up to the front porch. As her eyes studied the steps, she suddenly realized just how silent the property was. And then, the same feeling that had attacked her friend attacked her. "Amanda," she said in a whisper, "stop calling out."

Amanda turned in a rush and watched Sarah drop the backpack she was wearing to the ground. Before she could say a word, Sarah bent down and retrieved her gun. "I'm sure —I hope—" Amanda began to speak but stopped and kicked the ground with dismay and frustration. "Oh—I should have told you."

"Told me what?" Sarah asked, her eyes darting around and searching the land for any signs of human life or spying eyes.

"When you pulled into the parking lot, this horrible feeling swept over me—I should have told you," Amanda explained and grabbed Sarah's left hand. "I thought it was just nerves—maybe I should have listened to my gut. I'm sorry."

"You have nothing to be sorry for," Sarah promised. "Now, drop your bag and let's go inside and look around."

"Okay," Amanda replied, and quickly took off the backpack she was wearing and dropped it down to the ground. "I'm ready."

Sarah pointed to the front porch and cautiously climbed

the front steps. When she reached the top, she stepped onto a wooden porch lined with old rocking chairs that were weather-worn. The porch was clearly suffering from neglect and was in need of repair in many places. "Front door is closed," she pointed out, ignoring the condition of the porch.

"What should we do?" Amanda asked in a worried voice.

Sarah threw her eyes down at the floor and began searching for footprints. "The landing is dry," she said, in a disappointed voice. "No sign of anyone coming through here."

"Should I try the front door?"

"Yes," Sarah said in a careful voice. "I'll cover your back."

Amanda squeezed her hands together, drew in a deep breath, and then walked up to the large, thick wooden door that a hungry grizzly bear couldn't break down. Instead of trying to break down the door, Amanda simply tested the doorknob. "It's unlocked," she whispered.

"Stand back," Sarah whispered back. She cautiously stepped in front of Amanda and, with her gun at the ready, she eased the front door open. The door let out a loud, agonizing groan as it opened, giving away Sarah's secrecy—assuming she had any to begin with. "Stay close," she whispered to Amanda.

"Like glue," Amanda promised and followed Sarah into a large front room full of dusty furniture, creaking wooden floors, a cold stone fireplace, warped bookshelves full of old books, and a wooden desk shoved into the far right corner. A single hallway led away from the front room to the rest of the cabin. Weak trails of sunlight fell through two front windows caked with dust and cobwebs, breaking into a space that smelled of dust and danger. "Not very lovely, is it?" Amanda whispered as she followed Sarah deeper into the room. This was far different from the cabin she and her husband had stayed in.

"No," Sarah whispered back. She stopped in the middle of

the room, looked around, and then focused on the front door. "Go shut and lock the front door." Amanda nodded her head and ran to complete her task. As Amanda closed and locked the front door, Sarah turned her attention to the hallway. "Where does the hallway lead to?" she asked, keeping her gun at the ready.

Amanda engaged a strong deadbolt lock and hurried back to Sarah. "From what Mr. Grayman told me, this cabin has four bedrooms, a main kitchen, dining room, two bathrooms and a finished basement. This cabin was once used as the main office to the research center that once stood here. I suppose what he called bedrooms were really offices."

Sarah bit down on her lower lip. "What kind of research center was housed here?" she asked.

Amanda shrugged her shoulders. "Mr. Grayman never told me that," she spoke honestly. "He simply gave me a brief history of the area. He's not much of a talker and neither was his wife, I'm afraid. They never seemed happy to talk. I never understood why. I assume it was because they were eager to retire to Florida."

Sarah continued to bite down on her lower lip as her mind began to latch onto questions that would have to be brought to light at a later time. "We need to check the cabin," she told Amanda. "Stay close." Amanda grabbed the back of Sarah's jacket and followed her down the long hallway. "We'll check the kitchen first and then work our way around."

Amanda felt a cold chill run through her heart. In her mind she saw an old man lying dead on a dusty kitchen floor with a knife plunged into his back. Her nightmare quickly became a reality when she walked into the kitchen behind Sarah and saw Mr. Grayman lying face down on the floor. Only the poor man didn't have a knife plunged into his back —he had been shot. In the back. "No," Amanda cried and threw her hands over her mouth as tears began falling from her eyes. "No, no! It's not supposed to be like this."

Sarah ran to the body, knelt down, and checked for a pulse. "He's dead," she told Amanda and bolted to her feet. "We have to get back to my jeep. Come on!" Sarah grabbed Amanda's hand and ran her back down the hallway and into the front room. She dashed to the front door, disengaged the lock, yanked the front door open, and ran out into bright daylight. "Don't bother with the backpacks," she ordered Amanda, making her way down the front porch steps.

"You can count on that," Amanda promised. When her feet reached solid earth, she took off at a full sprint, keeping up with Sarah. Together they hit the trail at a high speed and managed to reach the parking lot. As Amanda ran, she felt like a dark shadow was chasing after her—reaching for her—hissing in her ear and laughing insanely. When she saw Sarah's jeep, she put her feet into hyper-drive and ran for the passenger door but slid to a stop when she saw that all the tires on the jeep had been slashed. "No!" she yelled in an anguished voice.

Sarah quickly jogged around her jeep and then ran around the old truck. "All the tires have been slashed," she said, making her way to Amanda. She took a second to catch her breath. "Someone doesn't want us to leave."

"Our legs aren't broken," Amanda cried. "We can run out on foot. Let's go!"

Sarah gently grabbed Amanda's arm. "We don't know who is out there—who might be watching us this very second," she said, slowly navigating her eyes around the land that had suddenly transformed into a deadly obstacle course. "If we try to run out on foot, we could easily be killed and no one would find us. Also, there's that grizzly bear—and my gun is no match for that bear."

Amanda looked around the land. She felt a pair of hideous, cruel eyes watching her. "We wouldn't make it out by dark anyway," she said in a miserable voice.

"No, we wouldn't," Sarah agreed.

Amanda looked at Sarah with pleading eyes. "What do we do—please—what do we do?"

Sarah pulled Amanda into her arms. "I'm not sure," she answered in an honest voice.

"It's not supposed to be like this," Amanda cried. "All of our troubles were supposed to be over."

Sarah checked the tires on her jeep. "Whoever slashed these tires knew what he or she was doing. These tires weren't slashed by some common thug."

"Great," Amanda complained, and hugged her own arms. She walked her eyes around the landscape. "The killer could be watching us right this second," she said in a low whisper. The day had turned creepy and downright scary. The sun, even though sitting high in the sky, appeared cold instead of warm. The land now felt dangerous and unfriendly—the trees like giant prison bars keeping her locked inside a frightening cell.

Sarah leaned up from the back right tire and brushed at her pants. "Amanda, you said a man named Mr. Fields is—or was—Mr. Grayman's attorney, right?"

Amanda nodded her head. "That's what the poor guy told me."

"Did Mr. Grayman mention a first name?"

"Afraid not," Amanda told Sarah in a disappointed voice. "Los Angeles, are you thinking that this Mr. Fields is the killer?"

"I'm not sure," Sarah replied, studying the landscape. "We're absent a third vehicle, which could mean Mr. Fields might not have shown up at all."

"But Mr. Grayman assured me he was on the property when I called him from the gas station," Amanda insisted.

"Could be that Mr. Fields managed to escape," Sarah

suggested, even though her gut told her otherwise. With no clues to go on, she felt desperate to latch onto a theory that would help her mind focus on a concrete suspect.

"We didn't pass anybody driving up here," Amanda pointed out. "The gas station we stopped at was only a mile or so from the turn-off. There's no way Mr. Grayman's attorney could have made it down that quick."

Sarah nodded her head. Amanda was thinking like a cop, and that was a good thing. "Exactly," she said.

"Maybe Mr. Grayman drove down and picked Mr. Fields up? I mean, he did say he had his plane ticket in hand, right? So that means he was packed and ready to go. Maybe he was going to drive the lawyer back down the mountain afterwards."

"Then where is Mr. Grayman's luggage?" Sarah asked. She walked over to the old truck and looked down into the bed. All her eyes saw were some old shovels, some worn-down work gloves, an axe, and some scattered dirt that was damp in a few places, like it had been freshly dug up from somewhere along a trail.

"Luggage?" Amanda asked. She hurried over to the bed of the truck and looked down. "This doesn't make any sense," she said in a confused voice. There was nothing in the cab of the truck, either.

"Not yet it doesn't," Sarah agreed. She raised her eyes and studied Amanda's face.

Amanda thought and said, "I'm sure he didn't mean he was literally holding a plane ticket. I bet Mr. Grayman was hinting that he was anxious to leave as soon as possible."

"I wonder why?" Sarah asked.

"What do you mean?"

Sarah checked her gun and then turned her back to the bed of the truck. "Mr. Grayman and his wife lived here for many years, right?" Amanda nodded her head yes. "And before they arrived you said some type of research station stood on this property?" Amanda nodded her head again. "It doesn't make sense to me that Mr. Grayman's murder was random. It seems to me he was killed for a reason—by someone who considered him a threat. Maybe that's why he sent his wife to Florida ahead of him?"

Amanda let her mind soak in Sarah's words. She turned and studied the shovels and axe in the bed of the truck. "Why would he have shovels and a work axe in his truck?" she asked. "The trail leading to the hot springs is north of here."

Sarah kept her back to the bed of the truck. "It appears that Mr. Grayman was doing some digging. The axe might be for cutting roots."

"Digging?" Amanda asked. "What—do you mean for gold?" she struggled to joke.

"Or something else," Sarah replied. "What seems right to me, in my mind—at least for now—is that if Mr. Grayman was digging for something, whatever he was digging for might have gotten him killed." Sarah narrowed her eyes. "I wish I knew who this Mr. Fields was."

"Me, too," Amanda agreed.

Sarah walked her eyes back to her jeep. "We can try and crawl down on flat tires. The going will be slow, but we can try. I might tear up my jeep doing it, but I would prefer to keep moving rather than standing around in the open like this."

"I'm with you on that," Amanda said, in an enthusiastic voice. She ran to the jeep and began to jump into the passenger seat. But the sound of a distant chainsaw made her freeze. "Do you hear that?" she asked Sarah, as all the color in her face drained away.

Sarah locked her eyes on the exit road and listened. A couple of moments later, she heard a tree crashing down through the woods. From the sound of the crash, it seemed the tree that had been cut down was very large. "I think we've just been blocked in," she said, in a worried voice. "Someone doesn't want us leaving."

Amanda felt panic grip her heart. "What do we do?" she begged.

"If the killer is down that way, we go this way!" Sarah said. She grabbed Amanda's hand and began running back for the main cabin. Her legs struggled up the steep hill to the clearing. Every muscle in her body cried out as she pushed her way up the hill. When the trail leveled off, she strengthened her grip on Amanda's hand, drew in a second breath, and picked up speed. "We'll use the main cabin as headquarters."

"Just like the Alamo," Amanda whined, barely keeping pace with Sarah. When she saw the main cabin come into view, she felt a sense of relief wash over her. At least the cabin offered shelter, she thought as she hauled butt to the front of the cabin and raced up onto the front porch. Sarah grabbed their backpacks from the overgrown grassy field on the way.

"Hurry!" Sarah yelled, throwing open the front door. Amanda ran through the front door and slid to a stop in the front room. Sarah slammed the door shut, locked it, and then bent forward to catch her breath. "You okay?"

"I'm okay," Amanda said, breathing hard. "Out of breath—is all."

Sarah squeezed her gun and forced her back to straighten out. "There are two doors—a back and a front. We can secure the doors. It's the windows I'm worried about."

"At least—we're—inside—where it's safe," Amanda replied, trying to catch her breath. "We can't be—taken off guard if we're inside."

Sarah wasn't so sure of that, but she didn't voice her thoughts on the matter. Instead, she began walking back toward the kitchen. "I need to check the body again."

"What for?" Amanda begged.

"Plane ticket—identity—wallet—anything," Sarah explained.

"Oh," Amanda fretted, and chased after Sarah as her friend hurried back down the long hallway toward the kitchen. When she reached the kitchen, she saw poor Mr. Grayman still lying dead on the floor. "Poor guy," she whispered.

"Amanda, honey, check the kitchen. We need weapons. Like knives—ice picks—anything you can find."

"Los Angeles—I—" Amanda bit down on her lip. "Okay," she finally caved in.

Sarah understood her friend's reluctance to locate items that could be used as deadly assault weapons, but the situation was dire and called for drastic protective measures. "I'll check Mr. Grayman." Sarah sat her gun down on the floor and began searching Mr. Grayman's body. After ten minutes of searching, she picked up her gun and stood up. "He's clean. Not even a piece of pocket lint on him."

Amanda walked over to Sarah holding a butcher knife. "I found a few kitchen knives. I put them on the counter—no ice pick."

Sarah nodded her head. "The killer obviously knows this land, Amanda," she explained. "Unfortunately, the killer knows the land better than we do."

"How do you know that?" Amanda asked. She glanced down at the butcher knife she was holding and shivered. "Awful little creature, isn't it?"

"Yes, it is," Sarah told her friend and continued. "Since the moment we arrived—about an hour ago—the tires on every vehicle have been slashed and a tree has been cut down. That tells me the killer knows his—or her—way around this land and can navigate the land with ease. I could be wrong—I don't have any hard facts to back up my statement—I'm simply telling you what my gut is feeling."

"Your gut is very smart," Amanda said, in a worried

voice. "I wish your gut—and mine—we're both wrong—because my gut is telling me the same exact thing."

"I thought that might be the case," Sarah said, and let out a deep breath. "I—I'm wondering why the killer is trying to trap us in? I'm sure he—or she—could have shot us dead at any second. Why trap us?" Sarah walked over to an old wooden table, pulled out a dusty chair, and sat down. "It's very dusty," she pointed out. "Didn't the Grayman's keep this place up at all?"

"Mrs. Grayman didn't seem like a very happy woman when my hubby and I met her."

Sarah placed her gun down on the table. "June Bug, honey, how did you come across this place, anyway? Did you find it on the internet?"

Amanda walked over to the table and sat down next to Sarah. Her legs were aching, and she decided it would be wise to rest them while she could. "I was searching for hot springs on the internet. The Snow Creek Hot Springs and Resort was listed on a tourism site—though the website was outdated." Amanda tossed down the butcher knife and removed her coat, feeling sweaty and overheated. "The resort sounded romantic—secluded—even a bit mysterious. So I called and spoke to Mrs. Grayman. I made a reservation, got directions, and well—the rest is history."

Sarah's mind struggled to make sense of the situation. "I guess the Grayman's needed some form of an income, and didn't care if the guests never came back because the place looked dusty," she said. "How much did you pay to stay here?"

"For a three-night stay, my hubby and I paid a little over a thousand dollars."

"That's steep—especially for a place so remote," Sarah said.

"Don't worry, my dear hubby let me know that every single night," Amanda sighed. "I thought the resort was—

well—a real resort." Amanda stopped rubbing her legs. "So what if I was overcharged? The land alone was worth more than the measly amount of money I paid. So what if my hubby fussed—I enjoyed every second. The hot springs were simply delightful—the land breathtaking—and we even made a campfire on our last night. During those three days, I fell in love with this place."

Sarah felt her heart break. She loved her best friend and wanted her to be happy. It hurt to see her dear friend's dream shattered all over the floor in the form of a dead body. "I'm sorry, June Bug. I really am."

"So am I," Amanda sighed. "But hey—I might still be able to buy this land—right?" she asked, in a weak, pale voice.

"I don't think your husband will allow it," Sarah told Amanda in an apologetic voice. "Sorry, honey."

"You can't blame a husband for protecting his wife, I guess," Amanda replied, and offered a weak smile.

Sarah patted Amanda's hand, grew silent, and let her thoughts wander around a bit. After a couple of minutes, she asked, "Amanda, honey, did you see a lot of the Grayman's while you were staying here?"

"Oh—only for breakfast and dinner. Every morning and every evening, Mrs. Grayman would bring food—eggs, pancakes, coffee for breakfast—beans, cornbread, chicken and rice for dinner. Real wilderness food. Not that I minded. Mr. Grayman told me over the phone what types of food would be served. That was part of the charm—although maybe it should have also been a red flag. But did I pay attention? No."

"Stop kicking yourself, honey."

"Oh, I can't help it," Amanda nearly cried. "I turned a romantic week into a bothersome holiday for my hubby, and now, because of me, I've trapped us in a bear cave. I admit that my hubby had every right to complain—but near the end of our holiday, he admitted that the land made up for the lumpy beds and bad food. He actually smiled, if you can believe that. Before we left, I took a walk—alone—and really fell in love with the land. And the potential of what it could become. Then, when Mr. Grayman told me he was selling, my heart nearly came out of my chest."

Sarah patted Amanda's hand again. "I'm sorry, honey. I really am."

"Be sorry for that poor old man, not me," Amanda told Sarah, and wiped a tear from her eye. "He's the one that was killed."

"And we have to find out why," Sarah reminded Amanda. "I'm still a cop—a retired cop—but a cop, nonetheless. I can't turn my back on justice just because we're in a tight squeeze. The last thing we need to do is act like two terrified, helpless women running through the woods tripping all over themselves. We need to be smart and stay smart. Whoever is outside is trying to push our panic button. Panic is the last path we need to run down."

"Maybe we should try the phone in the front room then?" Amanda asked, trying to find courage to replace her fear.

"We can try, but my guess is the line has already been cut." Sarah grabbed her gun. "Get your knife."

Amanda reluctantly took ownership of the butcher knife again and stood up. "Ready," she said, and carefully followed Sarah back into the front room. Sarah made her way to the old desk and picked up a black telephone. "Dead?" Amanda asked.

Sarah nodded her head. "No dial tone," she said, and placed the phone down. "Maybe there's an old CB radio around?" she asked, and looked back toward the hallway. "Maybe in the basement?"

"Oh no—no basement for this lady," Amanda objected. "I'm not going down into a dark basement and risk being murdered in a horrible underground lair. No ma'am."

Sarah bit down on her lower lip. "We have to find a way

to reach the outside world," she told Amanda. "I'll go search the basement. You can stand guard up here."

Amanda fretted again. "Oh, Los Angeles, what are the chances you'll find anything of use down in the basement? Please, don't go—don't leave me alone."

Sarah took Amanda's hands. "Honey, we're trapped, and we need to find a way to reach Conrad. The station back in Snow Falls has a CB radio. If I can find a CB radio here, we might have a chance."

Amanda knew Sarah was speaking the truth. She looked down at the butcher knife and then back up at Sarah. "Please hurry," she begged.

"I will," Sarah promised. "Now, show me where the basement door is located."

As Amanda walked Sarah back into the hallway, a shadowy figure began draining all the gas from the jeep and the truck in the parking lot. "No one leaves," the figure announced, and looked toward the entrance trail with sad eyes. "No one."

chapter three

Sarah pulled open a heavy wooden door. The door moaned and cried, it fought against being disturbed, but finally surrendered. "I don't know how long I'll be," she told Amanda.

Amanda peered past Sarah's shoulder and looked down into a dark, cold hole. She watched her friend reach into the darkness and managed to find a light switch. A pale, weak light flashed on, the light from a single bulb hanging from a bare wire. "Are you sure about this?"

"I'm sure," Sarah promised. "I'm sure the Grayman's wouldn't risk being trapped here with only a telephone. Even if the phone line is underground, that doesn't mean it can't be damaged. An animal could dig up the line—a hard freeze could hinder it—anything. It would make sense that a man Mr. Grayman's age would have a backup communication device somewhere—at least I hope so."

"Please hurry," Amanda begged.

"I will," Sarah assured her scared friend. "We have the front and back door secured. If someone tries to enter that way, they'll knock over the chairs holding the pots. If you hear anything, yell out and I'll come running."

"The doors may be secure, but what about the windows?"

Amanda worried. "I know we checked every single lock, but still—oh, now this place is giving me the creeps."

Sarah felt pity rise in her heart. She patted Amanda's hand and made her way down a steep set of wooden steps that delved down into a cold, windowless, concrete basement. She paused at the bottom of the stairs and looked to the left and then to the right. The basement extended the length of the cabin and was filled with old boxes stacked here and there. "Please let there be a CB," Sarah begged, and decided to check the right portion of the basement first. She walked over to a stack of three boxes and examined them. The boxes, to her curiosity, had a strange design on them. Under the design was a name, "Viral Green," she read the name aloud.

"Los Angeles, what is it?" Amanda called down.

"I found a stack of boxes with a design and name written on them," Sarah called back. "Viral Green is the name written on the boxes. The design looks like—a straight line with a—crooked 'Y' on it."

"Maybe the boxes belong to the research lab that once stood here?" Amanda asked.

Why would the boxes be in this basement? Sarah asked herself, and then called up to Amanda, "Could be." Sarah bent down, placed her gun in the ankle holster attached to her right ankle, and then carefully opened up the top box and looked inside. "Glass beakers," she whispered. "Why would Mr. Grayman have glass beakers in his basement?"

"Los Angeles?" Amanda called down again, "Where are you?"

"I'm checking out one of the boxes," Sarah called up to Amanda. "The box is full of glass beakers."

"Beakers?" Amanda asked. "Like in science experiment stuff?"

"That's right," Sarah called out. "How are things up there?"

"Silent," Amanda said, and shivered all over. "I feel like a fly caught in a spider web—waiting for the spider to show up at any second."

"Stay brave, honey," Sarah pleaded. She picked up a glass beaker and examined it in the weak light. "This beaker has been used," she whispered, spotting a grimy green residue stuck to the inside of the glass. She placed the beaker to her nose, sniffed it, and then yanked the beaker away as if it had stung her. "Awful smell."

Sarah placed the beaker down and looked around. "I'm going to walk deeper into the basement. Hang tight."

"Hang tight," Amanda mumbled under her breath. She leaned away from the basement door and studied the empty hallway. In her mind, she saw Mr. Grayman stand up in the kitchen, look in her direction with furious eyes, and let out a loud and creepy cry. "Stop it—stop it—stop it, Amanda! You're better than that," Amanda scolded herself.

Sarah didn't hear Amanda chastising herself. She walked deeper into the basement and began investigating one box after another. Each box had the same design and name. Some boxes contained copper wiring and pipes. Other boxes contained more beakers and plastic tubing that looked like silly straws.

When Sarah reached the back of the basement, she was shocked to find a small chemist laboratory setup, complete with a long table set up with what appeared to be a mad science experiment straight out of the movies. A wooden desk was shoved into the corner of the basement. Sarah headed straight over to the desk and checked the drawers. "Empty," she said, in a disappointed voice. But her disappointment was short-lived. A small box sitting under the desk caught her attention. "What do we have here?" she asked. She bent down, pulled the box out, and sat it on the desk. "Let's see." Sarah opened the box and nearly fainted. Two glass tubes full of liquid material were resting in what appeared to be a miniature steel rack. Each tube had a large red "X" on it. A slot for a third tube was vacant. "Oh—my," she whispered in a panicked voice and quickly backed away from the desk and ran back to the stairs. "Amanda!"

"What's wrong?" Amanda cried out.

"I found some sort of a lab—and a box holding glass tubes full of a strange yellowish liquid. I'm not sure if the liquid is some kind of virus or not?"

"Get out of the basement!"

"I—" Sarah felt panic rise in her chest. She hadn't located a CB, but feared the yellowish liquid she had found. "I'm coming back up!" she called out, forcing her mind to think rationally.

Amanda heard Sarah running up the stairs. As soon as Sarah was safely back in the hallway, she slammed the basement door shut and locked it. "What in the world is going on?" she begged.

"I think I might have an idea," Sarah said, breathing hard. She pointed toward the kitchen. "I think Mr. Grayman was more than just a harmless old man making money off a hot springs." Sarah reached down and retrieved her gun. "I think Mr. Grayman was a scientist—a virologist maybe?"

"Oh boy," Amanda replied. "Los Angeles, we have to get out of this place."

Before Sarah could say a word, a shadow appeared in the kitchen door. "You can't leave," a woman's voice announced. Amanda screamed and nearly fainted. Sarah spun around and aimed her gun at the figure. "I'm not your enemy."

"Get down!" Sarah yelled. "Now! Get down!"

"Or what?" the woman asked. "Will you shoot me? Perhaps that would be a mercy."

"Down—now!" Sarah yelled again. Instead of obeying, the shadowy figure turned and walked back into the kitchen. Sarah looked at Amanda and ran down the hallway. When she reached the kitchen, she saw a very lovely woman wearing a red and brown flannel shirt that hung over a long gray skirt standing over Mr. Grayman. "Who are you?" she demanded, keeping her gun at the ready.

"Nobody," the woman responded in a sad voice. She slowly turned and looked at Sarah with teary eyes. "This man was once a very dear friend."

Sarah stared at the woman. She stared into a lovely face scarred with misery, or so it seemed. "Who are you?" she demanded again. "I want a name."

"My name is Noel McGee."

Amanda stepped up next to Sarah and saw a woman with long black hair looking down at her hands. The woman resembled a sagging puppet that would never smile again. "Did you kill Mr. Grayman?" she asked, trying to sound tough.

"No," Noel replied and raised her eyes—brilliant eyes that could easily deceive even the most skilled detective.

"Then who did?" Sarah demanded. "I want answers."

"If you are told the truth, you will certainly die," Noel promised Sarah. "Sadly—you could be dead already."

"What do you mean?" Amanda gasped.

"The basement," Sarah whispered. "Those tubes I found—that liquid—it's a virus, isn't it?"

Noel nodded her head yes and spouted confusing, meandering phrases. "The basement is a grave." It was as if she was playing a game rather than speaking about reality.

Sarah felt her hands begin to shake. She had just begun a new life with Conrad and now she was being told her life was over. "What kind of virus is down there?" she asked.

Noel looked down at the dead body lying at her feet. "The worst kind," she whispered.

"Please, give us answers," Amanda begged. "I came here to buy this place and—"

"You were brought here to be a carrier," Noel interrupted Amanda. "You and your husband were both brought here to be carriers."

"I don't understand!" Amanda begged. "I found this place on a website for crying out loud!"

Noel nodded her head. "A deception," she explained. "They had to stay hidden from the government."

"Who?" Amanda nearly screamed. "Who had to stay hidden?"

"Viral Green," Sarah whispered.

"No," Noel corrected Sarah. "Viral Green was once housed in this very location, but the government shut them down."

"Then who?" Sarah demanded.

"In time, you will have your answers," Noel replied. "Right now, the man who killed Mr. Grayman is still at large. He managed to escape just before I arrived."

"We didn't pass anybody traveling up here," Amanda pointed out. "There are only two vehicles in the parking lot and—"

"There is a hidden trail that leads into this place," Noel told Amanda. "You can travel the trail on motorbike or four-wheeler."

Sarah lowered her gun. "You—slashed the tires on my jeep and—cut down the tree we heard fall."

"Yes," Noel admitted. "I also drained the gas out of each vehicle in the parking lot."

"Why?" Amanda snapped. "We need to—" Amanda stopped talking as her brain latched onto the obvious. "We could be sick—contagious—is that it?"

"Yes," Noel placed her hands behind her back. "I can't risk anyone leaving—and that includes myself. We could all be infected and contagious."

"Could be?" Sarah asked.

"There is always a chance we aren't sick. There is a chance the man who killed Mr. Grayman didn't release the virus."

"The third tube was missing," Sarah whispered to herself.

"The third tube was stolen," Noel confirmed in a whispery

voice that barely carried across the kitchen. "The virus has no smell. It can be altered into a mist and sprayed in the air." Noel looked at Sarah. "If we are infected—we'll know in the next forty-eight to seventy-two hours."

"Then what?" Amanda begged. "Do we die if we are infected?"

"If we are infected with the virus—once it incubates within the bloodstream—we will all die within twenty-four hours," Noel explained.

Amanda broke out into tears. "Oh, Los Angeles," she cried and hugged Sarah. Sarah fought back her own tears and wrapped her arms around Amanda.

"I'm sorry," Noel said, her voice sincere. "I tried to get here as quickly as I could—to stop him."

Confusion gripped Sarah's mind. "That man's wife—"

"I'm afraid she managed to escape to Europe."

"Europe?" Amanda wiped at her tears. "But she was supposed to be going to Florida and—" Amanda kicked herself for being so naïve. "And I bought right into the lie."

Sarah slowly let go of Amanda. "You said Amanda and her husband were brought here to be carriers?" she asked. "Please, explain. Why didn't they get sick on their first visit?"

Noel walked to the kitchen table and sat down. "There is a secret terrorist group at work, ladies," she explained. "The terrorist group known only as White Cell is housed all over the world. We don't know how many people belong to the group and who they really are—they are a secret society named after the white blood cells in the body. Why? Nobody knows." Noel looked down at her hands and continued. "Twenty years ago, when I was just beginning my training as a virologist, I came under the care of Dr. Grayman. I was assigned to this very location as an employee of Viral Green."

Sarah eased into the kitchen with Amanda. "Keep talking."

Noel nodded her head. "Dr. Grayman was a very brilliant

virologist until—sadly, he went against the policies of Viral Green, which, at the time, was being funded and managed by a secret government agency hidden inside of the CDC." Noel shook her head. "I was the person who contacted my supervisor and told her that Dr. Grayman was conducting unauthorized experiments. Dr. Grayman found out. He tried to kill me, but I managed to escape. He vanished into thin air before he could be captured." Noel looked at Sarah. "He vanished with a great deal of supplies, research papers—and viruses."

"Why in the world did he come back here?" Amanda asked.

"Viral Green tore down the compound and closed up shop. Only this cabin was left standing. This location would be the last place anyone would look for Dr. Grayman. Of course, his real name isn't Grayman. His real name is Werner Kraus. I'm simply calling him by the name you know."

"Let's call him by his real name," Sarah ordered Noel.

"Very well."

Sarah felt her temper flare. "So, who are you? Who do you work for? I want answers."

"I want to know if my husband is infected!" Amanda yelled. "You said we were brought here to become carriers!"

"Your husband is not infected," Noel promised Amanda. "Dr. Grayman—Kraus—backed out at the last minute. That's why he was killed. He couldn't go through with the orders given to him by someone in the White Cell."

Sarah ran her hand through her hair. "Why would Dr. Kraus even tell Amanda that a research station once stood here?"

"He did?" Noel asked, in a confused voice, her eyes wide and spooked.

"He sure did," Amanda proclaimed. "He was going to sell me this place, too."

Noel stared at Amanda. "Dr. Kraus didn't obey his orders

—he would have needed traveling money. At the same time, he would have wanted to leave an obvious trail to expose an agent in the White Cell group—of course, that has to be it."

"Are you implying the man panicked and was planning to run?" Sarah asked.

"Yes," Noel stated. "That is how it seems to me." She pointed at Amanda. "You and your husband were simply guinea pigs who managed to escape death due to one man's conscience. Why you came back—"

"I fell in love with this land, okay?" Amanda said, and wiped the last of her tears away. "When Mr. Grayman—Dr. Kraus—told me he was putting this resort—death trap, rather —up for sale, I melted. I guess he saw a sap and took advantage of me."

"Dr. Kraus was always very good at reading people," Noel explained. "He must have seen that you were beginning to care for the land and saw an opportunity to acquire the traveling money he needed."

Sarah looked down at the dead body. The only question in her mind was who shot and killed Dr. Kraus. Where was the killer now? And would he be back? If the man came back to try and kill them, that would mean he hadn't sprayed the virus into the air. He would have simply left to let the virus do the dirty work for him. For the first time in Sarah's life, she pleaded for a killer to return to the scene of his crime. "Come back," she whispered in a shaky voice, "please come back."

Night arrived. Noel made a pot of coffee and sat back down at the kitchen table. "Thank you for helping me carry the body into the next cabin," she told Sarah and Amanda.

Amanda was standing next to the back door. Her mind was solely on her husband. "Are you certain Dr. Kraus didn't infect my husband?" she asked Noel.

"If Dr. Kraus had obeyed orders, he would still be alive," Noel confirmed in a voice that set Amanda's worries at ease —at least for the time being.

Sarah stood next to the kitchen counters and watched coffee pour into a foggy pot. The smell of the coffee filled the kitchen air and slowly began destroying harmful thoughts. "Noel, who do you work for?" she asked.

Noel sat in silence. When she did answer Sarah's question, her voice was low and hidden. "I cannot reveal that."

"Obviously, someone must know that you're here," Sarah told Noel. "Please, we need to try and reach our husbands. If we are infected, we have the right to say goodbye to the people we love."

"I have no communication device on me and, unfortunately, no one knows of my current location. I am believed to be in Europe."

Sarah folded her arms. "You said there is a hidden trail. You must have a motorbike or four-wheelers hidden someplace. We can—"

"You must not try and leave," Noel ordered Sarah. "Even if you did try—the four-wheeler I arrived on has been destroyed by the man who killed Dr. Kraus."

"Then why did you disable my jeep?" Sarah snapped. She quickly caught her tongue and apologized. "I know why—to prevent yourself from leaving. I'm sorry I snapped at you."

"It is understandable," Noel assured Sarah. "Please, sit down."

"The man who killed Dr. Kraus could return. I would prefer to remain standing."

"If the killer does not return, its lights out for us," Amanda told Sarah in a sad voice. "I never thought I would punch the clock out this way—and it's all my fault. I was so stupid to have come to this—this ugly grave."

"How could you have known the truth?" Noel asked Amanda. "You were simply a pawn. Dr. Kraus returned back to the very location he had escaped from, transformed his lab into a hot springs retreat, and camouflaged himself under a new name. Not a single person knows the truth." Noel's voice became defeated. "Not a single person at Viral Green—within the government—the CDC."

"How did you find out that Dr. Kraus had returned?" Sarah asked. "And why didn't you inform anyone?"

Noel rubbed her nose. "I spent years searching for Dr. Kraus," she began to explain as the coffee pot continued to fill. "My searches never returned a positive lead. Eventually, I decided to go underground and attempt to locate Dr. Kraus through back channels. I had no choice, and I began working for the White Cell terrorist group."

"You what?" Amanda gasped.

"As a researcher," Noel confirmed. "I had one single contact—a voice that I never met. However," Noel added, "all of my research had to be sent to a certain P.O. Box in Los Angeles. I left my home on the East Coast and traveled to Los Angeles. I monitored the post office where my research was to be picked up. When I spotted a woman picking up my research package," Noel stopped rubbing her nose, "I followed this woman to a private cottage in the upper canyons. I'm not proud to admit this, but I viciously attacked her. After I subdued this woman, I tied her down inside the cottage and spent twenty-four hours collecting information from her—through very painful techniques."

"Torture," Sarah said.

"I'm afraid so," Noel said, feeling shame burn in her cheeks. "This woman confessed very important information that allowed me to track down Dr. Kraus. I immediately left for Alaska, but when I arrived, I was greeted by two gunmen who met me outside of the Anchorage airport. I was placed in a van and driven to a remote location, shot three times in the back, and left for dead."

"Oh my," Amanda gasped.

"As you can see—I am alive," Noel told Amanda.

"How?" Sarah asked. "You would have been checked for a protective vest."

"I was checked," Noel confirmed. "But you must understand—I actually work for very powerful people, and I was prepared." Noel reached out her right hand and touched her back. "I was wearing a flesh vest."

"A what?" Amanda asked.

"A vest that resembled flesh. It is very thin and extremely difficult to detect. The bullets I was shot with bruised me but did not otherwise harm me. I played dead and then managed to escape," Noel explained. "Because I was believed to be dead, I knew I had a certain advantage and began making my way directly toward this location. However, it was winter, and the weather conditions were extremely harsh. It took me two weeks to reach this location, and by then, Dr. Kraus and his wife were gone—taken away out of precaution and returned when spring arrived."

"You're a spy, aren't you?" Amanda asked, and shook her head. "Whatever happened to the days of women staying home, raising a family, cooking a good old-fashioned meatloaf dinner, and spending their evenings knitting a sweater? Or just getting a normal job instead of getting into espionage?"

"I wish those days still existed," Noel sighed. "I wish, more than you could ever know, that times were simple again. I regret my life and the choices I made."

Sarah stared at Amanda. "We'll talk about regrets later. Continue with your story."

Noel nodded her head. "I spent the winter in this location. When spring arrived, I knew Dr. Kraus would be returned under special guard, at least until it was confirmed the location was secure and clear. Dr. Kraus hated to be crowded and insisted he be left alone with his wife." Noel looked at the coffee pot. "Before I left, I bugged the phone line." Noel kept her eyes on the coffee. "May I have a cup of coffee please?"

"Sure," Sarah said. She picked up a brown coffee mug and filled it with coffee. "June Bug, coffee?"

"Sure, why not?" Amanda told Sarah.

Sarah handed Noel her coffee and poured Amanda a mug. "Hot," she said.

"Got it," Amanda promised and took the mug of coffee with grateful hands. "Did you find anything while you were here?" she asked Noel.

Noel took a sip of her coffee and nodded her head yes. "Research papers, letters, a personal journal. It wasn't long before I realized Dr. Kraus was being held hostage by the White Cell. The White Cell had managed to capture his daughter and take her hostage."

"I feel bad for his daughter, but sorry if my heart doesn't bleed for the man," Amanda told Noel and took a seat at the table.

"How did you know Dr. Kraus would return when spring arrived?" Sarah asked, pouring herself a mug of coffee.

"Dr. Kraus wrote down the date of his return in his journal," Noel explained. She set down her coffee. "I must confess that I became very ill that winter and nearly died. My resources were limited—food was scarce, and the frigid cold was not my friend. I spent my time in the basement next to a small heater eating very little food. I couldn't let my presence be detected. When I left, I made it appear that animals had managed to enter the kitchen and get at the food. I was fearful that my footprints in the cabin would be found, but to my relief they were not."

"And you found information out how?" Sarah asked.

"By listening to the phone conversations," Noel explained. "I arrived here with very little at my disposal. After I was shot and left for dead, I had difficulty finding even what I'd arrived with." Noel looked down at her coffee. "The device I placed on the phone was the one item I managed to keep on my body when I was shot. The device is very unique and allows a person to dial a certain phone and keep the phone line open without being detected. I could hear every word spoken in the cabin and every word spoken through phone calls."

"Just like a cell phone when it's turned off," Sarah pointed out. "You transform the cell phone into a private listening device without the owner knowing."

"Exactly," Noel said.

"You must work for some very powerful people."

Noel lowered her eyes. "Not anymore," she promised. "Dr. Kraus is dead. Now I can rest."

Sarah stared at Noel. "Dr. Kraus was more than just a close friend who turned on you, wasn't he?"

Noel sat in silence for a very long time. Then she raised her eyes. "He was my adopted father," she confessed. "He raised me as his own. After he tried to kill me—two years ago to the day—I found out an awful truth." Noel squeezed her hands into two tight fists. "My parents were scientists. Both of my parents worked with Dr. Kraus. On a very cold and rainy night, their car ran off a cliff. My parents were killed. Dr. Kraus was the driver who ran my parents off the cliff. I was eighteen at the time and had just begun my studies as a virologist in Norway—and, and," tears began dripping from Noel's eyes. "Dr. Kraus is dead—that's all that matters. It seems that in the end, he couldn't let the monster he had become kill millions of innocent people after all. At least he had some form of a conscience."

"Oh, don't cry, Noel," Amanda begged. She stood up and put her arm around the woman. "It's okay."

Sarah watched Amanda shower Noel with care and concern. Then she felt her own heart melt. "I'm sorry for all that you've been through," she told Noel. She walked over to the woman and rubbed her shoulder with tender hands. "I can't imagine."

Noel looked up at Sarah and Amanda with tear-soaked eyes. "I'm sorry that we all may die within the next two days. I—also want the man who killed Dr. Kraus to return, but I doubt that he will. Dr. Kraus was ordered to release the virus, and he failed. The man who killed Dr. Kraus knew you two were set to arrive. I'm certain he sprayed the virus in the air."

"Mr. Fields—the fake attorney," Sarah said, in a shaky voice.

Noel nodded her head. "I'm afraid so."

Amanda sat back down and took a sip of coffee. She had walked off alone and cried until it hurt after helping Noel carry the dead body into a separate cabin. Now she felt strangely calm about dying. After all, Jesus was surely waiting for her. "So—we wait," she said.

"We wait," Noel agreed.

"We wait," Sarah agreed. As a homicide detective, she had spent years coming to terms with her own mortality. The danger of being killed was an enemy she faced daily. But now, trapped in a cabin waiting to see if she was going to be murdered by a lethal virus—she felt scared. "I always assumed I would be killed by a bullet," she confessed. "Noel—how will this virus kill us?"

Noel looked up at Sarah with worried eyes. "You don't want to know," she promised. "What's important is that the virus can only be spread through human contact—sneezes—blood, that sort of thing. If we die in this remote location, there is a chance the virus will die inside of us. The virus matures in a warm bloodstream and cannot survive outside of the body for long."

Sarah walked to the back door and tapped the doorknob with her hands. "I wish I could have said goodbye to Conrad. The last thing I told him was not to forget to feed Mittens. Mittens is my dog." Sarah felt tears sting her eyes. "We've faced so much—and now it ends in a way I never would have expected. I honestly believed that my battle with the Back Alley Killer was my last."

Amanda stood up and walked over to her best friend. "At least we had some good shopping days," she tried to joke but failed. "Oh love, I know how you feel. Every time I think of my husband or son, I—I can't handle the thought. I've been praying my heart out—that's all I can do."

"Me too," Sarah confessed. She looked at Amanda and forced a smile on her face. "Maybe we should have let that grizzly bear eat us after all."

"What grizzly bear?" Noel asked.

"Oh, while we were driving up, this mean old grizzly walked out onto the road," Amanda explained. "Sarah had to throw our sandwiches out the window in order to make him move."

"He was a very large bear," Sarah added. "If that bear would have attacked my jeep, Amanda and I wouldn't be standing here right now."

Suddenly a strange smile came over Noel's face. "Old Ralph," she whispered.

"Who?" Amanda asked.

Noel looked at Amanda. "Old Ralph," she smiled again. "Old Ralph has been around these parts for years. When I worked with Dr. Kraus I would see him down at the lake hunting for fish or standing in the river catching salmon. He never bothered me, and I never bothered him. After a while—well, as strange as it may sound—that bear became like a friend to me. I never traveled very close to him, but at times he would just look at me as if to say he understood how I was feeling."

"I wish Old Ralph would have stopped us from coming up here," Amanda sighed. She sat back down at the kitchen table and grabbed her coffee. "I could really go for a cinnamon roll and a shopping trip right about now." Amanda looked at Sarah. "If we live through this, I'm going to go straight home to open me a dress shop and I'm never leaving Snow Falls ever again."

"Don't be so hard on yourself, June Bug," Sarah told Amanda and decided to sit down and rest her legs. "A dress shop can become very boring—at least now we're having an adventure, right?" Sarah sighed. "Our very last adventure, I'm afraid."

The kitchen grew silent. The three women each looked down at their coffee mugs, each thinking their own thoughts. What they didn't know at that time was that the same set of deadly eyes was watching the cabin. "I'll finish this one way or another," the voice hissed and scurried into a far cabin where he hunkered down for the night.

As the night became long, Sarah took the first watch as Amanda and Noel tried to sleep. She spent the four hours of her watch struggling to think about Conrad. But for some reason, all she could see in her mind was a hideous snowman wearing a leather jacket and chewing a candy cane. *I got you in the end, didn't I, Sarah? Oh yes, I did.* The snowman laughed all night long.

chapter four

Sarah eased into the kitchen and found Noel sitting at the kitchen table drinking a cup of coffee. Noel wasn't sitting like a person enjoying a normal morning cup of java. The woman was sitting tense and upset. Sarah assumed the woman was upset and distraught over their situation. Yet, she noticed, as she walked into the kitchen, some other heavy burden appeared to be pushing down on Noel's shoulders.

"Good morning."

"Good morning," Noel replied, and fought back a yawn. "Everything is still quiet."

Sarah nodded her head. She felt tired, wanted a hot shower, a clean change of clothes, and a decent meal. Her hair felt messy and her face, instead of lovely and beautiful, felt scarred by deep worry. The last thing she wanted was to be trapped in a remote location, possibly dying from a deadly, invisible virus. Sarah wanted to be home in her cabin, sitting in a warm kitchen in the presence of a loving husband, talking over a plate of hot pancakes. Instead, she was locked in a dusty kitchen surrounded by darkness and misery. But through her own worry and fear, she managed to catch a new burden that had attacked Noel during the night. "Is anything the matter?"

Noel took a sip of coffee. "I've been thinking," she told Sarah in a low voice.

"Let me have a mug of coffee and we'll talk." Sarah quickly poured herself a mug of coffee and sat down at the table. "Amanda is still sleeping. She had a bad dream—I didn't have the heart to wake her."

Noel kept her eyes low. "Amanda is a good friend. You're very blessed to have her in your heart."

"That woman has saved my life many times," Sarah explained. "I wish—I could save her life." Tears immediately stung Sarah's eyes. She let out a deep breath. "When my husband divorced me, I left Los Angeles and moved to Snow Falls—really not knowing what to expect but—needing to begin a new life for myself away from everything I knew. I met Amanda, and we immediately became the best of friends. We've been inseparable from day one. I love her in a way that I can't explain." Sarah looked toward the hallway. "That woman is more special than words can say."

"I'm sure she feels the very same way about you," Noel suggested. "A good friend doesn't give her heart to ugly creatures."

"I suppose not," Sarah agreed. She raised her eyes and focused on Noel, who looked miserable. "You mean—you don't have any friends?"

"Once upon a time I did, long ago," Noel confessed without making eye contact with Sarah. "Once I had family and friends. But then I turned bitter and pushed away everyone I'd once called a friend. I became a loner, determined to kill the man who murdered my parents, and becoming much like the monster he was in the process." Noel finally raised her eyes. "I became a very cruel woman, Sarah. I—don't deserve friends."

"I wouldn't say that," Sarah offered. "You were hurt and angry over the death of your parents. When you lose people you love, the heart grieves—and becomes angry, and even bitter. You set your mind on killing a monster. That doesn't make you a horrible woman, Noel. It makes you human."

"This coming from a homicide detective who has witnessed the very worst people can do to one another," Noel pointed out.

"I've seen my share of murders and those murders still haunt my dreams," Sarah explained. "I've seen the evils of man's heart running free across a city full of a lost people trying to find themselves. And through it all, somehow, I managed to maintain my sanity—by faith in Jesus and nothing else. But there came a time for me to leave that city and relocate to a quiet location and begin healing. Perhaps if we live through this, you will find a place to begin healing as well."

Noel put her coffee mug down. "I'm worried that we may be the first of many victims," she confessed. "The White Cell won't rely on the virus spreading from three people who may never leave this location alive. I fear that the man who stole the virus will release it into a large location—such as Fairbanks or even Anchorage. Once the virus is transformed into a mist-like form, it can be sprayed into the air at any location—undetected."

"Isn't that the objective of the White Cell to begin with? To spread the virus?" Sarah asked, confused.

"In a controlled environment," Noel pointed out. "The virus is meant to be used as a weapon, to target a certain enemy." Noel locked eyes with Sara. "Alaska was to become a science experiment, so to speak. The White Cell wants to understand how the virus lives within a certain environment —how fast it spreads—how quickly it actually kills. Right now, test results are the only eyes and ears they have into the virus. It is believed that it takes twenty-four to forty-eight hours for the virus to mature, and once the virus matures it will kill its victim within a twenty-four-hour time period. That is the primary data—hard data—that has been collected.

In reality—no one can actually predict how a virus will react once activated. Every living person is different—each body is different. Is any of this making sense?"

"Yes," Sarah nodded her head. "Continue."

Noel looked around the kitchen. "Amanda lives in a small, rural town. The town was chosen to become a testing ground. But when Dr. Kraus failed to infect Amanda and her husband, the White Cell came down hard on him, and Amanda was lured back to this location to be sprayed with the virus, as you know."

"Tell me why you believe the man who stole the virus will infect a large city," Sarah put down her coffee. "Will the White Cell order him to do so?"

Noel shook her head no. "The White Cell would not risk a global epidemic that they cannot control," Noel explained. "If the virus can be weaponized—which is the end goal—they can control governments. No more war, no more bombs or guns—fear will be the ultimate weapon. However, they will present their weapon—the virus—on battlefields to make their enemies fall into submission and then fear will become power."

Sarah bit down on her lip. "Noel, the US government has been conducting secret experiments on the American public for many years. I'm aware of an experiment that was carried out in the New York City subway that made hundreds of people very ill. In 1975, the government contaminated Los Angeles with a new strain of flu that made three-quarters of the city sick."

Noel nodded her head. "You are speaking the truth."

"How is it that the government isn't aware of the virus that was stolen? It's been my understanding that the government is the one creating deadly viruses to use in global warfare. Surely someone—anyone—would be aware that Dr. Kraus was operating a secret virus lab in Alaska."

"Sarah," Noel explained, "the White Cell is a terrorist

group—a group composed of hidden people from many different countries. Like Russia, Canada, England, Switzerland and China, and we're talking about shadow agencies that deceive their very governments."

"For example?" Sarah asked.

Noel hesitated. "I can't tell you more than that."

"Why?" Sarah asked. "I'm going to die anyway, right?"

Noel looked into Sarah's worn-down face. The woman deserved to know the truth. "The CIA is an intelligence agency," she told Sarah in a calm voice. "Within the CIA are shadow agencies—spies who work under an invisible cloak, following different agendas. The CIA has no way of controlling these people because they are undetectable. The world has become so tangled up in secrecy that no government agency can trust another—even in the same country. The FBI is always at war with the CIA, and the CIA is always at war with the Defense Intelligence Agency—it's a very vicious cycle. And in other countries, the same plague continues."

"I've heard rumors," Sarah told Noel. "When I worked in Los Angeles as a homicide detective, I heard lots of things."

Noel took a sip of coffee. As she did, her eyes went to Sarah. The woman impressed her. Sarah was a normal woman with a healthy fear of death, but she was also a fighter —a thinker—and a person who didn't go down in the first round. Sarah was also a woman who understood how to divide the truth from crazy conspiracy theories; and the truth was that there are dangerous people in the world who spread evil from ruthless hearts. "You cannot track the White Cell," she told Sarah. "It is impossible." Noel took another sip of coffee. "The White Cell began within the League of Nations and transferred their poison to the United Nations after the League of Nations dissolved. It's a cover for all their movements across world borders. The White Cell has infected world banks, world governments—and even small-town police stations."

Suddenly, Sarah froze. "Did you say—small-town police stations?" she asked, in a weak voice.

Noel nodded her head. "The White Cell has people everywhere and—"

"Noel," Sarah said, "my husband—he's a detective in Snow Falls. He told me last week that a new deputy was due to arrive in town after one of our long-time deputies decided to move his family to Fairbanks." Sarah put down her coffee. "Amanda visited the hot springs with her husband—and then a stranger arrives in town," she whispered to herself. "Could the stranger belong to the White Cell?"

Noel listened to Sarah whisper to herself. "It's very possible," she answered. "The White Cell might have sent someone to be a monitor."

"A monitor?" Sarah asked.

Noel nodded her head. "This person would have been inoculated with the antidote, something to protect him from the virus." Noel felt sadness enter her heart. "Yes, I'm sure that could be the case."

Sarah looked at Noel with worried eyes. "Noel, what will this person do now if Amanda and I—don't return to Snow Falls as infected subjects?"

"Leave," Noel replied. "The person sent to Snow Falls would have no logical reason to stay. Certainly, the White Cell would cancel his mission and relocate him."

"Unless," Sarah stated in a desperate voice, "a new person was injected with the virus." Sarah felt confusion grab her mind. "Why would the person who stole the virus release it into a large city? Why would this person go against his orders? Wouldn't the White Cell kill him?"

"Exactly," Noel pointed out. "The person who killed Dr. Kraus and stole the virus certainly knows that he risks the possibility of elimination—as I mentioned, White Cell is composed of people from every nation. There is even betrayal and murder within the ranks of the White Cell itself. It is very possible that the man who stole the virus might have taken a very high pay-off. I'm certain this man was injected with an antidote." Noel stopped talking for a minute. "Sarah, my thoughts are only an assumption. It is very possible the man who stole the virus will obey orders and take it to whatever location he was ordered to."

"I hope you're wrong," Sarah told Noel in a shaky voice.

Noel nodded her head. "Me, too." Fortunately, what Noel didn't know was that her assumption was wrong. The man who stole the virus and killed Dr. Kraus was still very close by, lurking in the woods—waiting and watching.

Sarah grew very silent as her mind contemplated a horrible thought. "Noel, let's assume you are wrong—and let's assume the White Cell takes another course of action—such as infecting the entire town of Snow Falls. Is that possible?"

"Yes," Noel answered honestly.

Sarah hit the table with her fist, nearly spilling her coffee, and then stood up. "We can't just sit here like this. We have to act. There has to be some way to contact my husband."

"There is no way," Noel told Sarah in a disappointed voice. "However," she said, trying to add a hopeful note, "if seventy-two hours passes and we are still alive—then perhaps we can leave."

"You don't believe that."

"No," Noel confessed. "You were left alive for a reason—you and your friend were left alive to return back to your town. You two will act as the invisible 'spray.' The tools with which the White Cell infects your town—at least, that was the plan. I prevented you from unknowingly killing innocent people. However, I didn't catch the man who killed Dr. Kraus. I failed, and for that, innocent people will die."

"Don't give up the fight yet, sister," Sarah begged. "There

has to be a way. You're a virologist for crying out loud—you have to know of a way."

"The virus that could be maturing within us, Sarah, is very deadly. If we are infected—and we let out a single sneeze—" Noel shook her head. "We cannot leave this location."

Sarah felt extreme frustration rattle her nerves. "There has to be a way."

Guilt racked Noel's lovely face. "I failed to capture the man who stole the virus. I'm sitting here worrying if this man will betray his mission and infect millions or obey his orders. If this man infects millions—it will be all my fault. At least I can keep us secure at this location, and prevent us from making anyone sick." Noel looked at Sarah with desperate eyes. "There is too much confusion, uncertain variables, and assumptions. We're fighting a powerful group of terrorists who won't hesitate to kill each other; killers who want world domination through murder—cold-blooded murder. The virus that was stolen is nothing more than a machine gun that will gun down innocent people. I tried to snatch the machine gun." Torment captured Noel's voice. "But I failed."

"Did you?" Sarah asked. She ran over to Noel and bent down. "Did you fail?" she asked again and grabbed Noel's hands. "You're just one person, Noel—a very brave person who threw her punches as hard as she possibly could. You didn't fail—because you cared enough to act. Those who know the truth and don't act—those are the people that fail."

Noel felt tears begin to fall from her eyes. "I let a killer escape with a virus capable of killing millions."

Sarah pulled Noel into her arms and held her the way only a true friend could. "Noel, honey," she whispered, "we can't give up the fight," she begged and then, without understanding why, her mind began to think about the basement. "Noel," she asked, "why didn't the killer steal all of the tubes? Why just one?" she asked, in a confused voice.

Noel leaned up and looked at Sarah. "I've been wondering about that myself. And I don't have an answer."

Sarah stared into Noel's watery eyes and pulled the woman into her arms again as her detective mind went to work.

Amanda wasn't keen on the idea of Sarah and Noel going back down into the basement. She wasn't keen on wearing the same clothes she had worn the day before, either, but all she had in her backpack was some silly resort wear that was not enough to keep her warm in the drafty, deserted lodge. But most of all—she wasn't keen on the idea of dying. That is why she agreed to stand guard at the top of the stairs while Sarah and Noel ventured down into a dark hole. The idea, Amanda was told, was to see if Noel could try and create an antidote herself. The idea was a reach because Noel assured both Sarah and Amanda that she didn't have the resources to create an antidote. Sarah insisted that Noel had to at least try. Amanda agreed, even though she secretly agreed with Noel. "I'll stand guard," she promised, as Sarah and Noel descended into the basement.

Sarah made her way to the back of the basement and showed Noel the miniature steel rack holding two tubes. "The third tube is missing," she pointed out.

Noel picked one tube up and studied the liquid inside. "I know," she said. "I explored the basement before you arrived."

Sarah backed away from Noel. "Who do you truly work for?" she asked in a voice that was calm only through significant effort. "Noel, we need to be truthful with one another."

Noel carefully returned the tube she was holding back to its place in the rack. "Sarah, I can never tell you who I work—

worked for. You wouldn't understand if I did—and you would hate me."

"Try me," Sarah challenged Noel.

Noel walked over to the lab bench and studied the equipment with doubtful eyes. "Do you really want to know the truth about me?" she asked.

"Yes."

Noel kept her eyes on the table. "Very well," she said, and slowly began to allow the truth to trickle out. "I worked for a private agency within the CDC specializing in viral ecological warfare. There is a very long complicated name that was assigned to my area specialty, but to make it simple, just think of it as viral ecological warfare. Viruses designed to kill and infect plants and crops."

"I appreciate it. Long, complicated names get me tongue-tied."

Noel hesitated and then continued. "Dr. Kraus was the leading virologist in viral ecological warfare. That is, he was assigned to this area of the world."

Sarah leaned against the work desk and folded her arms. "You were trying to create a virus that would kill crops and plants in order to create famines in other countries, right?"

Noel felt guilt sting her heart. "My parents were virologists," she explained. "I was brainwashed into believing I was—performing a beneficial service for my country. But, yes—I was part of a secret agency trying to create a virus that would starve millions. A virus that would lie dormant when sprayed and be activated only using a secondary chemical agent."

"And did you?"

"Dr. Kraus did—however, he altered the virus to attack the human immune system instead of vegetation. I don't know why he did that. Maybe it was simply an accident of science. The virus—if we are infected—has to mature under certain temperatures inside of the body." Noel finally raised her eyes. "The virus enters the body in a frozen state. Once it comes to body temperature, to state it in simple terms, it hatches, if you will, and comes to life, reproducing and devastating the body in a very short time."

"I understand," Sarah assured Noel. She looked down at her hands for a minute and then raised her eyes and focused on Noel. "I can see why a terrorist group like the White Cell would want the virus. The virus, once sprayed, according to you, is odorless, tasteless, and undetectable. The perfect weapon."

"I fear my enemy succeeded in acquiring the virus."

"Maybe," Sarah sighed, and pointed at the table. "Noel, you have to find a cure—please try," she begged.

"Sarah," Noel replied, keeping her voice calm, "look around. There is not enough equipment, tools and data present in this basement to begin a research project. Antidotes usually take years, sometimes decades to create! If there was adequate equipment, it would still take me weeks—months really—to even get remotely close to creating an experimental cure."

"But you worked on this virus with Dr. Kraus. You have to know—"

"I worked on a virus that was being created to kill vegetation—not humans," Noel pointed out. "He took that last step without me."

"Maybe so, but you seem to know a lot about this virus we may be infected with," Sarah fired back.

"Enough to scare me—yes," Noel confessed. "But not enough to create a cure. You see," Noel explained in a very scared voice, "the virus inside of us—it's like a chameleon, it adapts and changes when it detects a threat, making it nearly undetectable. Sarah, Dr. Kraus was a genius. He wasn't some random doctor pulled in off the street. When he was ten years old, he began his higher studies in Switzerland. Albert Einstein would have been envious."

"He must not have been too smart if he allowed himself to be shot and killed," Sarah told Noel.

"Dr. Kraus became involved with a very deadly terrorist group that no one escapes from—that was his one mistake. Dr. Kraus had one weakness—pride. He always protected his pride with money. Money was power, and power destroyed those who insulted his pride."

"Dr. Kraus is worm food now," Sarah pointed out. "I don't mean to sound so crude, but that awful man deserved a bullet." Sarah pointed at the table. "Come on. You have to try."

"I'll only waste what valuable time we have left," Noel sighed, "but I'll explore each box in this basement and see what I find. Perhaps I'll come across something of use."

Sarah nodded her head. "It's better to take action rather than—" Suddenly, Sarah stopped talking. A strange look came over her face.

"What is it?" Noel asked, alarmed. "Are you feeling ill?"

"No, no. I feel fine," Sarah promised. "I was just wondering why this location was chosen to begin with." Sarah turned and looked north. "Close to the hot springs, I mean." Sarah rubbed her chin. "You said Dr. Kraus was a genius. Surely the man had some say in the location Viral Green chose to build their research center, right?" she asked herself. Sarah continued to rub her chin. "Surely Dr. Kraus was in charge of the research station—and chose this location for a reason."

"That's a possible assumption," Noel told Sarah. "This location is very remote."

Sarah looked at Noel. "But why choose a location close to a hot springs?" she asked.

Noel shrugged her shoulders. "I honestly never thought of that. I used to take walks to the hot springs when I worked here, but Dr. Kraus never showed any interest—at least not to me. As a matter of fact, I can't recall him ever even mentioning the hot springs at all."

"But there has to be a reason," Sarah insisted. "And there has to be a reason why the killer only stole one tube of that deadly virus instead of all three." Sarah reached down and removed her gun from the ankle holster. "I'm going to take Amanda and walk to the hot springs. I need to do a little investigating."

Noel became nervous. "Please, do not try to hike out of here," she begged.

"I wouldn't dare try to leave," Sarah promised. "However, I do believe that we may be barking up the wrong tree. I believe all of our talk is leading us in the wrong direction."

"What do you mean?" Noel asked.

"It is possible that the new deputy in Snow Falls is this monitor you mentioned. And that Amanda and I were brought here to become unwitting carriers for the virus and return back to Snow Falls. But it's also possible that the killer might not be as far away as we think." Sarah pointed at the steel rack holding the last two tubes. "Why didn't the killer take all three? And why was Dr. Kraus shot in the kitchen and not in the basement? Why did the killer leave his body out for anyone to find?"

Noel placed her hands down on the table and shrugged. "When I arrived, Dr. Kraus was dead."

Sarah walked over to Noel and touched her shoulder. "Noel, I know there is a lot that you're not telling me—things that you'll never share. I'm sure the people you are working for now are not the same people you worked for at the CDC."

"Sarah, I—"

Sarah held up her hand. "My concern is my best friend and seeing my husband again. Now, if we are infected, that means time is slipping away and we have to act." Sarah pointed down at the table. "You get to work down here, and

Amanda and I will get to work topside. We still may have a chance."

"Not if we are infected," Noel insisted.

"Even if we are infected," Sarah promised. "Don't you see?"

"No—I don't," Noel begged. "Sarah, I am considered a woman with a dangerous amount of intelligence. But right now, I feel very dumb. All my mind can think about is dying. I deserve to die for my crimes—and I will before I ever hurt anyone again. But I don't want to die." Tears began falling from Noel's eyes. "What chance, what hope do we have? I did what was required. I crippled any chance of escape. I trapped us here, and the three of us will die here together."

"Will we?" Sarah asked. She walked Noel away from the table and back to the stairs. "You said the virus has to live at a certain temperature before it can mature, right?"

"Yes."

"You said the virus enters the human body in a frozen state, right?" Sarah asked.

"Sarah, winter is still—"

"Maybe winter is still an arm's reach away, but the hot springs aren't," Sarah insisted. "Dr. Kraus, if he was as smart as you claim, must have chosen this location for a reason. Maybe," Sarah said, in a desperate voice, "he did so because of the hot springs. Maybe—somehow or someway the hot springs can kill the virus."

Noel stared at Sarah in shock. Then, as if a soothing, clean rain dropped from the sky and began washing away the fear blinding her intelligence, she began to understand, or so she pretended. Sarah noticed a sudden look she couldn't identify flash through Noel's eyes and then vanish just as quickly as it had arrived. "The human body stays within an acceptable temperature range—but—if we can raise the body temperature, hmm."

Sarah pointed back toward the far corner of the basement,

too concerned with saving her life and the life of her best friend to focus on the sudden strange look that had come over Noel. "That's for you to find out," said Sarah. "We may or may not be infected, and playing around with the virus could kill us if we're not already infected—but we have to take that chance. Now, go get to work."

Noel drew in a deep breath. "It could be possible," she said, in a calm voice. "It could be possible that if the body temperature is raised beyond a certain level, the virus would die." Noel spun around and looked at all the stacked boxes. "Go, leave me alone and let me get to work."

"I will," Sarah said, "but please stay alert. Amanda and I will be outside and there will be no one upstairs to stand guard."

Noel nodded her head. She patted her waist. "I have a gun."

"Use it," Sarah warned Noel and hurried up the stairs.

"What's happening?" Amanda asked, reading Sarah's face.

"I'm not really sure," Sarah told Amanda in a strained voice. "My mind is still struggling to make sense of this mess." Sarah closed the basement door. "I'm certain Noel is hiding many secrets from us, but what I'm sure of is that she's not kidding around about the virus. If she thinks the killer sprayed the virus in this cabin, we have to believe her."

"But?" Amanda asked, looking deep into Sarah's eyes.

Sarah grabbed Amanda's hand and pulled her into the front room. "There are two leftover tubes down in the basement. Why didn't the killer steal them? It doesn't make sense to me. Surely if the killer came here to kill Dr. Kraus and infect us with the virus—surely he would have stolen all three tubes and not just one. Something had to have happened." Sarah studied the front room. "There's no sign of a struggle, but that doesn't mean that Dr. Kraus didn't put up a fight. Also," Sarah pointed out, "why was the body of Dr. Kraus left out in the open?"

"I don't know," Amanda confessed. "I've been too busy thinking about my family—my hubby and son—to focus on this horrible place."

"This horrible place just may save our lives," Sarah promised Amanda. She pointed toward the basement. "I think it's possible that Noel might have arrived sooner than she's letting on, and she may be hiding a few secrets about the killer from us. I don't want to push her, though," she warned Amanda. "The woman is on the verge of a mental breakdown—I have to keep her focused and on track."

Amanda bit her thumbnail. "I like Noel," she said, in a low whisper, "but it does seem she is hiding a lot of truth from us. But, I wholeheartedly agree that she is about to fall off the edge. I also believe she is very serious about us being infected."

"Noel has obviously been through more than anyone should have to endure," Sarah agreed. "Whoever she is working for seems to be just as deadly as the White Cell terror group." Sarah shook her head. "We may never know the full truth, but right now we need to focus on the hot springs."

"The hot springs?" Amanda asked, confused. "This is hardly the right time to go take a relaxing dip."

"I'm not interested in taking a hot dip—at least not yet," Sarah promised. She walked over to the front door and, with her gun at the ready, cautiously disengaged the lock and pulled the door open. Wonderful, sweet, fresh air rushed into the stuffy room and struck Sarah in the face. Sarah closed her eyes for a second, soaked in the soothing air, and then stepped out onto the front door. Amanda quickly followed. "We have to be careful," Sarah cautioned Amanda. "The killer, or killers, could still be close by."

"Love?" Amanda asked, still confused.

Sarah studied the beautiful landscape and looked toward

the river. "I don't think the killer has fled the scene," she explained. "And I don't think the killer wants us dead, either. If that were the case—we would be." Sarah kept her eyes focused on the land as a refreshing wind touched her tired face. "There's more than meets the eye, June Bug, and we have to find out what. And time isn't on our side—on anybody's side for that matter."

Amanda turned her eyes out toward the land and, even though she was scared out of her mind, she somehow felt a strange calmness wash over her. "Okay, love, I'll take us up to the hot springs and we'll poke around some. At what? I have no idea. But I think you do."

Amanda took Sarah's hand and carefully walked off the front porch. In the distance, a pair of eyes watched. "The hot springs?" the voice whispered. "Why are you going to the hot springs now?"

chapter five

Sarah followed Amanda down a long winding trail surrounded by tall trees, beautiful bushes, and lush landscape. In some places, the land opened up to a beautiful view of the mountain, while in other places, the trail squeezed to a narrow passageway. "It's very beautiful," Sarah told Amanda as her eyes searched for any sign of human movement.

"I know, love," Amanda sighed, climbing a small hill on the trail. She paused and looked around. "As much as I want to hate this land now—I can't," she told Sarah in a teary voice. "This land captured my heart and I—oh, I wanted to own it. I still do," she confessed, and wiped away a tear. "The property didn't make me sick—the evils of man did. Why should I hate this land for something a lousy terrorist bloke did to me?"

"If we survive this nightmare, we'll buy this place, June Bug, I promise," Sarah said. She checked the watch on her wrist. "If I don't call Conrad by tomorrow night, he'll jump in his truck and drive up here. Once he sees the tree down across the road, he'll know something is wrong." Sarah quickly wiped Amanda's tears away. "I made such a big fuss about being able to handle this trip—Conrad didn't want us going, and we had our first big argument. The last thing I told him was not to forget to feed Mittens." Sarah looked around. "He'll think I didn't call him last night because I'm still upset. He'll probably think the same tonight. But if I don't call him by tomorrow night, he'll drive up here."

"We could be dead by then," Amanda sighed, and dried up her tears. "If Conrad finds us before we're dead, he could become infected, too."

"I know," Sarah replied. "On the other hand," she added, "Conrad may not be allowed to leave Snow Falls." Sarah quickly explained about the new deputy. Amanda listened with dread. "That sounds very possible."

"I wouldn't doubt it," Amanda told Sarah and kicked at the ground with her right foot. "You should have never left Los Angeles, love."

Sarah checked her gun. "It was time for me to leave Los Angeles. I'm just sorry Pete changed his mind at the last minute and decided to stay. I guess I should have known." Sarah thought about her old partner and felt a smile touch her face. "Los Angeles gets into your system. When I was working as a homicide detective, I would have never dreamed of living in Alaska. If someone would have told me my husband was going to divorce me and that I was going to begin a new life in a little Alaskan town—I would have arrested that person and had them admitted to a mental hospital. Now look at me. Remarried, living in a small Alaskan town, and now I'm trapped in the middle of nowhere fighting to stay alive."

"I know what you mean, love," Amanda said, as they continued hiking. "I never dreamed of leaving London. London was my home. When my hubby told us we were moving, I was heartbroken. I cried for days." Amanda swept her eyes up and down the trail. "I didn't even know where Alaska was on the map. I was a city girl—fog and rain were my companions, and shopping was my passion. Oh, how many times did I stop off for a custard tart and a hot tea before exploring a new dress shop?" Amanda's eyes filled with warm memories. "In my day, London was special—so many sweet memories."

Sarah felt a smile touch her face. "There was an old diner that stood in front of the beach down a remote highway—way off the beaten path. I'm not sure if it's still there or not. Anyway, I would drive to that diner whenever I had the time to sit, drink coffee, and look down at the beach—the waves especially—and think about a new book I wanted to write—or not think at all." Sarah kept her eyes walking around and very alert as she talked. "I remember the smell of coffee, hamburgers cooking, and the sounds of the old jukebox playing songs from the 1950's. That diner was my special place, just like London was your special place."

"You're going to make me start crying," Amanda warned Sarah.

"Don't start crying," Sarah begged, "because if you do, I'll start crying and we'll never get anywhere and—" Sarah stopped talking. Without warning, she grabbed Amanda's arm and yanked her down to the ground. "There," she whispered and pointed to a tall tree. "I saw movement."

Amanda felt goosebumps crawl down her spine. She cast her eyes at the tree but didn't see anything. However, if her best friend said she saw movement, that was good enough for her. "Could it be Noel?" she whispered.

Sarah shook her head. "I saw a man, not a woman," she whispered. Then, to Amanda's shock, she took aim and fired a single bullet at the tree. "Whoever is behind that tree, come out!" she yelled.

Silence fell. Amanda kept her eyes on the tree and waited to be shot at. But then she heard someone start running off into the brush, away from the trail. Sarah started to stand up and give chase, but Amanda grabbed her arm. "Could be a trap," she warned.

Sarah considered Amanda's warning and nodded her head. "Smart thinking," she complimented Amanda. "I guess I'm more upset than I realized if I'm willing to go chasing a stranger through these wild woods."

"Don't kick yourself, love," Amanda told Sarah and rubbed her shoulder. "We're in a tight situation, and I, for one, know my mind isn't capable of thinking straight, never mind about roses and teacups."

Sarah eased up and looked out into the woods. "Whoever that man is, he didn't fire back at me. I didn't think he would."

Amanda dared to lean back up. She didn't like being out in the open like this, but she sure was curious to find out why her best friend had risked their lives. "Do tell, love."

"Whoever that man is," Sarah explained, "I think he's infected, too, and waiting to see if we find a cure." Sarah kept her gun at the ready even though she knew the strange man she had run off had no intention of returning—at least not for the time being. "One tube was stolen—not all three. That's the key, June Bug. Also," Sarah pointed out, "Dr. Kraus was left in the kitchen. That's the second key. And last," Sarah pointed out, "Noel went through a lot of trouble to make sure we couldn't leave. Why? All she had to do was explain the obvious—or even kill us. There's more to this story, June Bug."

Amanda studied Sarah's words. "Well, whoever was hiding behind that tree didn't kill us—" Amanda looked back toward the cabin. "You didn't seem very worried about leaving Noel alone, either."

Sarah nodded her head. "I think—and I could be wrong—that Noel is trying to keep me off-guard. She confessed to me earlier that she was afraid that whoever killed Dr. Kraus and took the virus might spray the virus in a large city. Her story didn't make sense to me. I mean, I suppose it's possible, but June Bug, as a trained cop, I felt that the woman was trying to make me look to my right instead of my left. And this whole business about the White Cell terror group—it's possible—but then again, maybe it's not. Maybe," Sarah said in a careful voice, "Noel is spinning lies in order to hide the obvious truth? I'm trying to process the facts and straighten everything out in my mind—and I admit that I'm hitting a lot of sharp edges—but I think I'm starting to see something tangible I can hold onto."

Amanda felt confused. "If you tried to spin this tale into a book, your readers would kill you."

"Tell me about it," Sarah sighed. She rubbed her temples. "I know Noel isn't a killer—and I believe she might be telling the truth about certain things—but, June Bug, the woman is—well, she's out on a very shaky limb talking to birds that just aren't there."

"Are you saying she's a nut?" Amanda asked.

Sarah shrugged her shoulders. "I'm saying I think she's been through more than a woman in her position can handle." Sarah reached into her front dress pocket and pulled out a small black device. "I checked the phone while you two were sleeping last night. I found this device. Noel did bug the phone." Sarah looked around. "I know she doesn't want to die—I feel she isn't a bad person—but she's trying to hide something from us. What? Maybe the man I shot at might be able to tell us. What I do know is that the whole White Cell terror group thing is—possibly not true. I believe the people Noel is working for are the true terror group and she's trying to protect their identity."

"Are you saying Noel is still a terrorist?" Amanda gasped.

Sarah bit down on her lower lip. "It's possible she found out who the people she was working for truly were and had a big change of heart? I don't know, June Bug. But right now I want to focus on the hot springs. Whoever was watching us will make his presence known soon enough—that is, if we make him think we have a cure. Come on."

Sarah took Amanda's hand and walked her the rest of the way down the trail. The trail ended at a large river with a gentle current. "This way," Amanda said, and pointed to her right. A small trail branched off to the right and ran beside the river. Sarah followed Amanda down the trail for a quarter of a mile and then, to her amazement, she saw what appeared to be two large pools sitting off from the river. The two pools had steam rising up from them. "There they are," Amanda said, and nodded toward a shallow part of the river. "We have to walk across the river to get to them."

"That's fine," Sarah assured Amanda. She rolled her pant legs up to her knees and stepped into part of the river that actually felt warm instead of cold. "It's very beautiful back here," she told Amanda, walking through the river and looking at the two pools of water. The two pools sat a few feet apart, feeding small streams of bubbling water into the river. The pools weren't very large in size and, Sarah thought, if a person wasn't looking for them, they could be easily overlooked.

"The hot springs look to be about waist deep," Amanda explained, trudging through the river.

Sarah glanced back over her shoulder toward the trail. She felt like she was in an entirely different world. She could scream at the top of her lungs and no one would hear her. There were no people, no traffic, no smog, no crime, no pollution—just natural, beautiful land, pure and untouched by the greedy hand of man. "If I can only figure out why Dr. Kraus chose this location," she whispered and focused back on the hot springs. "Is it because of the hot springs? Or did he find the hot springs by accident?"

Amanda listened to Sarah talk to herself. "Love, we're really far back. I'm not sure that evil doctor chose this land because of these two hot springs." Amanda stepped out of the river onto dry ground, turned, helped Sarah out of the river, and then walked to the closest pool. She bent down and touched the hot water with her right hand. "This is the pool my hubby and I sat in. Oh, it was so nice. We sat back here for over an hour, soaking, talking, drinking tea—all very romantic."

"I bet it was," Sarah agreed. She bent down and touched the hot water with her left hand. The water was indeed very hot. "These hot waters can make the body temperature rise," she whispered.

Amanda nodded. "I felt like I was ready to melt when I got out," she explained.

Sarah leaned up and looked around. She wasn't sure what to look for. All she knew was that there was something—some clue—that she had to find; some clue that would save her life and the life of her dear friend. "June Bug, Noel said Dr. Kraus vanished before he could be captured, right?"

"Yes."

"She also said he vanished with supplies, right?" Sarah asked.

"I believe so, yes," Amanda said.

Sarah looked into the woods. "I wonder if he buried those supplies close to the hot springs," Sarah continued to look around. "Noel said the virus enters your body in a frozen state."

Amanda focused on Sarah's thoughtful eyes. "Ah," she said, catching on, "but how cold, right?"

"Exactly," Sarah pointed out. "Maybe Dr. Kraus needed a natural cooler to keep his work cold—but cold at a certain temperature?" Sarah pointed at the river. "The water was warm where we crossed, but I'm sure it gets a lot colder downriver."

Amanda nodded. "Perfect refrigerator," she said.

Sarah walked back to the river and looked down at the rocky floor. "Hey, look. I didn't notice this before. The rocks we walked across," she noticed, "they aren't natural. Someone put those rocks there." And with those words, Sarah drew in a deep breath, placed her gun down on dry ground, walked back into the river, dropped down to her knees, and began pulling at the rock. The water rushed up to her waist but didn't overwhelm her. "Help me, June Bug," she begged Amanda. "We need to see what's under these rocks."

Amanda let out a painful moan, walked into the river, eased down onto her knees, and sighed. "I didn't think I was going to go for a swim today," she told Sarah, feeling the river soak her body from the waist down. "I suppose I did need a bath, though."

"The water actually feels nice," Sarah pointed out and managed to pull up a medium sized rock. "These rocks are very heavy. We're going to have to work as a team to remove them."

"Okay," Amanda said, drew in a deep breath, and went to work. An hour later, she hauled the last rock out of the river with Sarah and then began digging at the river floor with her hands. It wasn't long before her hands struck a wooden box. "Hey—hey—we found something!" she exclaimed in an excited voice.

Sarah felt relief wash over her heart. She had feared that the river was going to turn up only dirt. "Let's see what we found, June Bug," she said, in a quick voice. With much effort, she helped Amanda pull a box out of the river and onto dry land.

"A wet, waterlogged, muddy box," Amanda said, and plopped down on the ground, exhausted from all the work. Even though her body was tired, her voice still held excitement. "What do you suppose is in the box?" she asked Sarah.

Sarah sat down next to Amanda and wiped her hands on her dress. "I'm not sure," she said, and retrieved her gun. "One thing is for certain," she told Amanda. "That box is very important. The only question is, who hid the box under the river?"

"Dr. Kraus?"

"That's what would make sense," Sarah admitted. She searched the land for any sign of movement. "The box is secured with a lock. I think we should take the box back to the cabin and open it."

Amanda studied a rusted lock attached to the box. "I suppose we could try and break the lock with a rock?" she suggested. "But if we're being watched, we may not get very far with whatever's inside."

Sarah considered Amanda's suggestion. She wasn't in a hurry to break into the box right out in the open. If curious eyes were watching, she didn't want to reveal the contents of the box, assuming the box had any contents to reveal. She was used to exploring new evidence in a secured location such as a police station. However, Amanda's words reminded her that she was far from a police station, had very little time to live, and needed to hurry. "Okay," she agreed. "Let's break into the box."

Amanda searched around and found a rock about the size of her hand. She handed the rock to Sarah. "You can have the honors."

Sarah sighed. "Thanks," she said, and took the rock.

"Anytime, love."

Sarah crouched down on her knees, focused on the rusted lock, and then, with all the strength she had, began trying to break into the box. After striking the rusted lock over five times, the lock suddenly popped open, surprising both Sarah and Amanda. "Well," Sarah said and threw down the rock, "that wasn't too hard."

Amanda began to nibble on her lip. "Well—I suppose we should open the box," she said, in a nervous voice. In her mind, Amanda feared finding a deadly virus—far worse than the virus that might already be eating her body alive—growing in a slimy tube, waiting to be brought to life. "Be careful, love."

Sarah stared at the box and then reached out two nervous hands and cautiously pried open the lid and peered inside. "Look at this," she said, in a quick voice, and pulled out a journal wrapped in a plastic freezer bag.

"Oh my," Amanda gasped, "that looks like a—a man's journal."

"It could be the journal of one Dr. Kraus," Sarah said, in a careful voice. She quickly tucked the journal under her left arm and crawled to her feet. "Let's get back to the cabin."

"I'm with you," Amanda promised, and forced her legs to work. "Let's move," she said, in a hurried voice. "If we're being watched, I don't want to be caught out in the open like this."

Sarah nodded her head and carefully walked back through the river and waited for Amanda. Once Amanda was across, she jumped into a fast pace and made a swift path back toward the cabin. With each step, she expected the man she had fired at to jump out from behind a tree or bush and attack her. With each step, she expected to see the grizzly bear she had fed peanut butter and jelly sandwiches to burst out of nowhere and swallow her whole. When the cabin came into sight and no harm had come to them, Sarah breathed a sigh of relief and raced up onto the front porch. "Hurry," she urged Amanda.

"I'm hurrying," Amanda assured Sarah, and ran to a rocking chair and collapsed. "I need a tea and custard tart," she said, breathing hard.

Sarah sat down next to Amanda and took a minute to catch her breath. "And I thought walking the streets of Los Angeles was tough," she said, and rubbed her left ankle with her right hand. "I'm sore all over."

"A nice soak in the hot springs will help," Amanda replied and leaned her head back. "If we live to ever take a relaxing soak, that is."

Sarah kept her eyes alert and gazed across the land. At

this distance, the river sparkled in the sun, singing to a land glowing with beauty and sunlight. "It's such a beautiful day —it's horrible to have to hide from its touch in fear. I could pack a picnic basket, walk right out to that river, lay down a blanket, and sit under this sweet sun all day eating and reading."

"I know, love," Amanda agreed. She tossed her eyes toward the river and actually smiled. "Now you can understand why I fell in love with this land."

"Yes, I can," Sarah promised. "I can understand why it captured your heart because this place is capturing mine—the same way Snow Falls did." Sarah took the journal from under her arm and placed it on her lap. "I hope this journal will help us survive," she told Amanda. "I want to live to see winter—and then spring. I want to take a nice soak in the hot springs and have a picnic beside the river. I can see Mittens running and playing—"

Amanda heard tears beginning to form in Sarah's voice. "Love?" she asked, concerned. "Are you okay?"

Sarah shook her head no. "If we—die—Conrad and I—I wanted us to grow old together. I wanted to grow old with you—in Snow Falls."

"I feel the same way, love," Amanda promised Sarah and took her hand. "Your little shopping buddy isn't ready to kick the bucket, you know. I have a son and a husband—I have you and Conrad." Amanda wiped Sarah's tears away. "I want to die old and after a long, full life, too. I want to see my grandchildren and have my hubby drive me insane with his bell. I want to wash our gray hair away with lousy hair coloring and laugh about our aches and pains. I want to have a million shopping trips with you at O'Mally's and take our husbands to the bank." Amanda nearly began crying. "I'm not ready to die—but if Jesus wills it, then so be it. I just pray it's not our time."

Sarah looked deeply into Amanda's eyes. "How are you

feeling?" she asked. "Are you feeling any different? Sick—weak—dizzy headed?" Amanda shook her head no. "Me neither," Sarah replied. "Noel said the virus matures within a twenty-four to forty-eight-hour period. It's been almost twenty-four hours."

"I've been keeping track of the time," Amanda confessed in a painful voice. "I've been monitoring how I'm feeling. So far, so good, love. Maybe the virus wasn't sprayed into the cabin?"

"Don't count on it," a deadly voice said.

Sarah jumped and went for her gun. Before she could reach her ankle, a tall man built like a grizzly bear and wearing a black tactical assault uniform darted around the front porch. The man aimed a gun at her. "Take it easy," Sarah told the man.

"Not a word," the man said, and motioned for Sarah and Amanda to leave the porch and follow him. He lowered his gun and hurried down to the far cabin. Amanda looked at Sarah and shrugged her shoulders. Sarah bit down on her lip, studied the situation, and finally decided to follow the man. Amanda followed on worried legs. When she reached the far cabin, she saw the man step inside and vanish.

"He could have killed us," Sarah told Amanda, slowly approaching the cabin.

Amanda nodded her head. "I know, love."

"Use caution," Sarah urged Amanda and carefully stepped into a one-room cabin covered with layers of dust and time. She spotted the man sitting down on a wooden bed frame holding a bare mattress.

"Close the door."

Sarah helped Amanda into the cabin and closed the door. "Who are you?" she asked.

"My name is Nolan. That's all you need to know."

"Fair enough," Sarah replied. She eased Amanda close to her and then studied Nolan's shadowy face. The man appeared to be in his early thirties, had a military-style haircut, a face that was meaner than a rattlesnake, and eyes colder than ice. Yet, even though the man appeared tough, he seemed scared—not only scared—terrified. "Nolan, what do you want?"

"My wife," Nolan told Sarah, and pointed toward the main cabin. "I came here to save her life. But, instead," Nolan shook his head, "she won't leave."

Sarah looked at her friend. Amanda shrugged her shoulders. "Do you mean Noel? Talk to me, Nolan."

Nolan stared at Sarah. "Lady, I work for some very dangerous people who sent me here to kill a man and capture a virus." Nolan placed his gun down on the bed and ran his hands through his short hair. "I have a background in virology. That's how I met my wife."

Sarah waited for Nolan to continue. When Nolan fell silent, she asked, "Noel isn't well, is she?"

"Why should she be?" Nolan snapped at Sarah with a vicious tongue. "My wife has been shot and left for dead—more hits have been put out on her than you can imagine—she's been through one nightmare after the next." Nolan shook his head. "Why? Because she wouldn't give up trying to find Kraus."

"Nolan, Noel mentioned a terror group called the White Cell. Does that group actually exist?"

"Sure it does," Nolan said, with bitter confusion in his eyes. "Who do you think I'm working for?" Nolan locked eyes with Sarah. "She's a skilled deceiver. She doesn't want you to know that I'm her husband—that I was the one sent to kill Kraus and capture the virus. She's been twisting you around with half-truths and half-lies this entire time."

"I assumed."

Nolan nodded his head. "I figured," he told Sarah. He ran his hand through his hair again. "Noel was lying about that woman and her husband becoming contaminated virus carriers. And you were right about the new stranger in your town—he is a monitor." Nolan took a breath as if he needed to steady his mind. "Kraus didn't contaminate your friend and her husband as ordered. He had no intention of contaminating her after he assured the boss man he had devised a plan to bring her back. That's why I was sent here—to do the job for him."

"You ugly, filthy rat," Amanda spat.

"Hey lady," Nolan fired back, "I had no intention of contaminating you. I'm not claiming to be a saint, but I know when to stop hanging with a rough crowd." Nolan tapped his gun. "The boss man doesn't want to weaponize the virus and sell it to the top bidder anymore."

"He just wants to release the virus, doesn't he?" Sarah asked.

Nolan nodded his head. "Your little town was supposed to be a lab experiment. If the experiment went well—he was going to order the virus to be released in Los Angeles, New York, Paris, Lagos, Mumbai, Shanghai, and Tokyo—every city in America and abroad with a large population over a one-week span." Nolan shook his head. "I came here to save my wife, kill Kraus, and destroy the virus. Only—"

"Only what?" Sarah demanded. "Talk to me, Nolan."

"Yes, talk to us, you slime," Amanda growled.

Nolan glared at Noel. "My wife hates me. She will kill me on sight if she sees me. She—"

"She what?" Sarah ordered Nolan to talk. "What did Noel do? Did Noel release the virus?"

"No," Nolan snapped. "Noel came here to kill Kraus and destroy the virus. She was too late—so was I." Nolan stood up and pointed toward the main cabin. "I arrived before Noel and made my way toward the cabin through a back trail no one else knows. When I got close to the cabin, I heard a gunshot. I ran to the cabin and peeked through the window, assuming Noel had arrived before I did."

"Noel didn't kill Dr. Kraus," Sarah pointed out.

Nolan agreed. "I saw Dr. Kraus's wife standing over his body holding a gun—she was the one who killed the guy, not me. But—" Nolan shook his head. "The woman was holding a specially designed spray bottle that connects to the tubing the viruses are housed in." Nolan stared at Sarah and Amanda with confused, shocked eyes. "She just began spraying the air—with no concern or remorse. I—for the first time in my life, panicked. I ran for my four-wheeler, but when I arrived—someone had slashed the tires, cut the battery cords and drained the gas."

"Noel?" Sarah asked.

"It had to be," Nolan answered. "I panicked even worse and ran back to the cabin just in time to see Noel sneak through the back door. Before I could react, I heard a gunshot, and Noel had shot Kraus's wife." Nolan ran his hands over his face. "Noel is my wife—I love her. I knew she'd been exposed to the virus now—what choice did I have? I ran into the cabin. When Noel saw me, she tried to shoot me—I had to flee, knowing we were contaminated." Nolan removed his hands. "About two hours later, you two arrived."

"Where is Mrs. Kraus's body?" Sarah asked.

"I watched Noel hide the body in a hidden cellar under the kitchen floor. She began to hide Kraus's body in the cellar, but you two arrived before she could. She spent a lot of time in the basement, but I don't know what she was doing." Nolan shook his head. "I was too afraid to go back into the cabin—the virus—we're all contaminated." Nolan sat down on the bed and put his face into his hands. "We're all dead."

"Why didn't you come to us before now?" Sarah asked.

"I had to get a feel for your motives," Nolan told Sarah in a stern voice. "Time is short and I can't afford to align myself with enemies. Once I figured you were okay, I knew it was time to talk."

"Why?" Amanda asked, anguished. "We can't save you."

"Noel can," Nolan told Amanda. "She can save all of us—and only you two can convince her to save us. We have less than twenty-four hours." And with those words, Nolan grew silent with dread as the two women looked at him and contemplated their fate.

Across the overgrown field from where they stood, the main lodge held a growing darkness. Noel stood in the basement staring at the last two virus tubes, contemplating her next step amid doubt and confusion, as her tormented mind began to crumble away, sending her down a very dark and deep hole.

chapter six

Sarah's mind raced as she contemplated several ideas at once. Her gut told her to move quickly, but her cop mind told her to move carefully and evaluate their options first. "Does Noel have the virus Mrs. Kraus was spraying?" Sarah asked Nolan.

"I'm not sure," Nolan explained. He stood up and began walking back and forth. "The old lady could have sprayed out the entire bottle or had some left over. I didn't see Noel take the spray bottle into the basement—I didn't see the spray bottle at all, for that matter."

Amanda felt like screaming. "You said Noel could save us. Why wouldn't she admit that fact—that very important fact—that very, very, very important fact—to us?"

"Because she wants to die, and she wants to take you down with her," Nolan told Amanda in a hurt voice that seemed out of character for a man of his make. "She blames herself."

"Blames herself for what?" Sarah asked.

Nolan stopped pacing. "Noel is a certified genius," he explained, in a very serious voice. "She was chosen to work with one of the smartest men alive." Nolan walked back to the bed and sat down. "She helped Kraus develop the virus—

unknowingly. Kraus deceived Noel and when Noel's parents began to warn her about Kraus, Kraus killed them and used her sorrow to draw her deeper into his sticky web of lies. Without Noel, Kraus was nothing, and he knew that." Sarah folded her arms and listened. Nolan placed his hands together and continued. "Noel began having concerns about Kraus and began confessing them to me. I don't exactly know the entire story because I was working in Atlanta at the time. But what I do know is that Noel called the boss at Viral Green and spilled the beans that Kraus was breaking policy. It wasn't long after that when Kraus tried to kill Noel."

"Noel was telling the truth about that, then," Sarah said.

"Yeah, she was," Nolan agreed. "She was telling the truth about a lot of things she told you—mingled in with some deception. The truth is Noel doesn't want you leaving this place. She wants to die." Nolan shook his head. "In her mind—she sees me as the enemy. She honestly thinks I escaped with the virus. She thinks I sprayed the virus."

"Why?" Amanda asked.

"Noel always told me that she was very fond of old lady Kraus. She said the woman was like a second mother to her. Then she was forced to kill her. I think that finally pushed her over the edge. After losing her parents, Noel clung to Mrs. Kraus. It nearly killed her to turn on Dr. Kraus, even though she had no choice," Nolan shook his head again. "I'm assuming this is true because honestly, I don't know what's going on in Noel's head. I heard her tell you that she was worried I might spray the virus in a large, crowded area—disobeying direct orders from the White Cell and obeying the highest bidder. I kept wondering why she was telling you that. Then I realized she was deflecting blame. She was hiding her pain, and running from the truth."

Sarah stretched her back. Her mind felt exhausted. Trying to keep pace with Noel and Nolan while desperately attempting to discover the truth was very tiring. "Nolan, we'll come back to Noel in a minute. First, I want to talk about Mrs. Kraus. Why would that woman kill her husband and then spray the virus? Surely she must have known she was committing suicide?"

"Lady," Nolan said, "your guess is as good as mine on that one." Nolan reached into his pocket and snatched out a cigarette and a pack of matches. "You mind?"

"I mind," Amanda griped. "I may be dying, but I still care about my lungs."

"Tough luck," Nolan told Amanda with a dismissive roll of his eyes, and he lit up, blowing a huge cloud of smoke out into the already dusty, still air of the cabin.

Amanda balled up her fists, then relaxed. She walked over to Nolan and slapped the cigarette out of his mouth. "Learn some manners," she berated him. "We're all stuck in here. Have some compassion for your fellow man. You're lucky I didn't punch you." Nolan stared at Amanda in shock but didn't make a move in her direction. Instead, he ground out his cigarette and nodded his head, giving her a look of begrudging respect. "That's better," she said. "Thank you, Nolan."

Sarah sat down in a wooden chair and rubbed her face, trying to dispel the tension in the air. "Nolan, I found this journal. I believe it belongs to Dr. Kraus. It seems to be written entirely in German, at least from the first couple pages I glanced at."

"I saw you find the journal," Nolan told Sarah. "That's why I decided it was time to talk. I didn't know it was in German, but that makes sense—maybe Kraus was trying to hide it from Noel. She never learned the language, but I did, when I was stationed on an army base there. Maybe he wrote down a cure for the virus in his journal." He paused and rubbed a tired hand over his face. "Noel can save us—she knows how—but I'm not going to lay down and die just because she refuses to try, ladies. I worked as a virologist for ten years before joining forces with the White Cell in order to find my wife."

Sarah raised her head. She studied Nolan's face and then tossed him the journal. "Take your best shot."

"Love?" Amanda asked worriedly.

"If Nolan wanted us dead, we would be dead," Sarah told Amanda. "Sit down and let rest your legs, okay?" Amanda looked at Nolan with weary eyes and then plopped down in a wooden chair beside Sarah. Nolan nodded his head, opened the journal, and began to read. Sarah fought back a yawn and waited. Amanda began picking at her thumbnail. After a solid, tense half-hour passed, Nolan finally looked up from the journal. "What?" Sarah asked.

"Either Kraus is lying, or Noel is lying," Nolan said in a weak voice.

"What do you mean?" Amanda asked.

Nolan closed the journal. "It can't be—it just can't be. Kraus has to be lying—he has to be lying," Nolan pleaded.

"Talk to me, Nolan," Sarah begged. "What did Kraus write in his journal?"

Nolan closed his eyes. "Kraus wrote that Noel murdered her parents, then tried to murder him. He claimed it was Noel who was transforming the virus into a weapon to attack humans instead of crops and ecological targets." Nolan looked at Sarah with confusion. "Kraus claimed Noel used Viral Green to destroy him by claiming he tried to kill her." Nolan tossed the journal back to Sarah. "Kraus writes that he escaped with the virus, but feared Noel would never give up searching for him—that's why he went to the White Cell—for protection. Bad move on his part."

"Keep talking," Sarah ordered Nolan.

Nolan stood up and walked over to the cabin door. "Kraus assumed Noel would never return to this location. So he came here himself a few years later and began trying to find a cure for the virus Noel created. A cure. A cure!" Nolan stopped talking. He looked at Sarah. "Could it be old lady Kraus was spraying what she thought was a cure instead of a virus? Could it be we're not infected?"

Sarah felt her heart jump with hope. She stood up and looked around the room. "Nolan, what else did Dr. Kraus write?"

"In the final entry, he wrote that he feared Noel had located him, and he wanted to try and get his wife as far away as possible while he tried to hide his research," Nolan explained.

Amanda stood up and looked at Sarah. "That's why he sent her to Florida ahead of him. And one tube was missing—two remained," she said, in a curious voice. "Could it be, love, that those two tubes are the cure and not a virus?"

"Maybe," Sarah admitted, and drew in a deep breath. "It could also be that Noel came here to infect Dr. Kraus with the real virus, along with Mrs. Kraus." Sarah bent down and took out her gun. As she did, her head began to feel funny. She dropped down to one knee and placed her left hand on the floor.

"Love?" Amanda asked, and dropped down to her knees in panic. "What is it?" she asked.

"I don't know—all of a sudden I just became very dizzy," Sarah explained, and shook her head. "Please—help me stand up." Amanda helped Sarah stand up. "Better," Sarah promised. But when she looked at Nolan and read the concern on his face, she knew she wasn't better. On the contrary, she was far, far worse. "Nolan?"

"Dizziness is one of the first symptoms you experience when infected by the virus," Nolan said in a weak voice.

"No," Amanda cried, "no! We are not infected, we can't be! Mrs. Kraus—she had to have been spraying the cure—not the virus."

"Maybe Kraus didn't create a cure that just stops the virus," Nolan suggested. "Maybe he created a second virus to kill off the first virus, an infection to neutralize it. Remember, he was working for the White Cell. The boss man is a cruel person. I doubt he would have allowed Kraus to waste time and money working on a cure instead of a virus." Nolan stepped away from Sarah.

"Wait, wait, wait," Amanda yelled. She struggled to clear her mind while holding Sarah's hand. "Why would Mrs. Kraus shoot her own husband and begin spraying a virus in the air? None of this makes sense."

Sarah felt anger rise in her heart. She wanted answers but felt the weight of confusion eating at her mind. For a brief second, a theory made sense and gave hope. Now she was being kicked back down a dark hole. "Nolan, what do we do?" she asked, still feeling dizzy.

"Kraus didn't write anything down that can help us," Nolan complained, gesturing to the journal on the dusty bed. "All he did was turn the tables on Noel and point the finger at her." Nolan kicked the floor. "I was warned not to fall in love with her. I was warned that she was a very dangerous person."

Amanda looked at Sarah. "Love, I need some fresh air."

"Me, too," Sarah admitted. Grabbing the journal, she worked her way outside into the bright sunlight. As she did, she spotted Noel standing outside, a few yards away from the porch of the main lodge, searching the land. Sarah felt anger erupt in her heart, clearing away the dizziness. She drew in a deep breath, charged up to Noel, and pointed her gun at the woman. "You lied to us!" she yelled.

Noel stared at Sarah with calm eyes then looked at Amanda. When she saw Nolan following behind Amanda, the calmness in her eyes transferred into rage. "I will kill you!" she yelled.

"Shut up!" Sarah yelled. "You lied to us."

"I told you the absolute truth," Noel promised Sarah,

changing her voice into that of a victim. "That man is a hired killer. He sprayed the virus—"

"Put a lid on it," Amanda snapped. "I thought you were a friend—boy, was I ever wrong. You really pulled the wool over our eyes last night, sister."

Nolan stepped up beside Amanda. "Don't do this, Noel. Please," he begged. "I came here to take you away. To get you help."

"You betrayed me and allowed those men to shoot me in the back!" Noel spat. "I trusted you! You were supposed to be my husband!"

"I didn't know we were going to be betrayed!" Nolan yelled back. "I was sent to bring you in peacefully. I was assured your life would be spared if I helped capture you. What choice did I have? The boss man wasn't going to let you walk into this place and kill his top scientist, Noel."

Noel threw her eyes at Sarah. "Shoot him—please," she begged. "He has contaminated—"

"Stop with the lies," Sarah snapped. "Nolan told us that he witnessed Mrs. Kraus spraying the virus—or a cure—or something." Sarah held up her left hand and presented Dr. Kraus's journal. "We found this journal. Dr. Kraus confessed many interesting truths. Now, it's your turn to tell the truth."

Noel stared at the journal with poison eyes. "So he did manage to hide the journal after all," she hissed.

"I want answers," Sarah yelled. "I trusted you to help us find a cure."

"A cure?" Noel said, and then leaned back her head and laughed. "There is no cure, you idiot." Noel pointed a hard finger at Nolan. "You three have become my lab rats. It's too bad I had to kill Mrs. Kraus. I really did like her, but she decided at the last minute I wasn't paying her enough, and hid the virus she sprayed in the cabin from me."

"The virus—the real virus?" Sarah asked, trying to keep up.

Noel let a hideous grin cover her once lovely face. "Kraus was working on a virus that could kill my own. A virus that White Cell believed was deadly but was, in fact, harmless to humans. It was only deadly to my own little creation. Mrs. Kraus assisted me in switching out the viruses." Noel looked at Nolan and then back to Sarah. "I injected her with an antidote that protected her. I wanted to believe I could trust that woman, since she was like a second mother to me." Noel narrowed her eyes. "I was wrong. After that woman killed Kraus and sprayed my virus inside the cabin, she waited for me and demanded more money. I had no choice but to kill her."

"Noel, you're insane," Nolan said. "Why are you doing this?"

"To control the world. To control White Cell. To control everyone," Noel snapped at Nolan. "If my virus acts as I suspect it will on human subjects, then I will have absolute power. Mrs. Kraus may have managed to hide one of my tubes, but I still have two more and I am very capable of making more. You see, you idiot, the time arrived to kill Kraus and put my plan into action, and seek my revenge on White Cell." Noel glared at Sarah. "Kraus had to die because he knew my secrets."

"You killed your parents," Sarah told Noel in a disgusted voice.

Sarah's words slapped Noel across the face. "I had to. They were growing suspicious of me," she hissed. "When I confessed my plan to them, they threatened to report me to the CDC. My parents left me with no other choice."

"You are a sick woman, Noel," Amanda said. "Boy, last night we were holding you and wiping away your tears. You really played us like an old violin, didn't you?"

Noel looked at Amanda. "I will carry out my plan," she promised. "You three have less than forty-eight hours to live. You can run, but you risk infecting millions of innocent people. You have no choice but to stay and die. If you decide to stay, I will make your last hours on earth very comfortable and ensure you die as painlessly as I can." She smiled with sickly sweet malice.

Sarah balled her left hand into a fist and punched Noel in her face. The impact was sudden, fierce and powerful. Noel stumbled backward, dropped to the ground, and fell unconscious. "Nolan," Sarah said, in an urgent voice, "Noel wouldn't risk coming here without extra antidotes, right?"

"Maybe—who knows?" Nolan said, staring at Noel's unconscious body. "She—I saw them shoot her," he said, in an angry voice and before Sarah could react, he aimed his gun at her. "Drop your gun, lady!" he yelled. "I'm taking my wife and getting out of here."

"And risk infecting millions?" Sarah asked, shocked. "No way!"

To Amanda's horror, she watched Sarah aim her gun at Nolan and wait. "Now—everyone calm down," she begged.

"If you try to leave, I'll be forced to shoot you, Nolan," Sarah warned.

"I'm taking my wife and getting out of here," Nolan yelled and held his ground. "Fire if you have the guts, lady," he dared Sarah and waited. Amanda closed her eyes and began to pray.

"You're not leaving," Sarah warned Nolan. "Now please, we can get through this. I need you to start searching the property for the antidote. Maybe Noel hid a vial of the antidote someplace? Amanda and I will check the cabin and—"

"No deal," Nolan yelled. "Once I take Noel from here and get her to understand what I've done for her—saved her from assassination—I'll be able to convince her of my love. She'll come around and inject me with an antidote," Nolan narrowed his eyes. "That woman is my wife. I'm not deserting her. She needs serious mental help and I'm going to see that she gets all she needs."

"And risk killing millions?" Sarah asked, incredulously. "No deal."

"Then shoot me," Nolan dared Sarah again.

"Enough!" Amanda screamed. She spun around and pointed a hard finger at Nolan. "Take your wife and get lost, pal. I hope you have a swell honeymoon because you're going to be dead before it even starts." Amanda threw her finger at Noel. "If you think that woman is ever going to accept you as her husband again you're barking up a dead tree. But that's none of my business. So just take her and go. Sarah and I have an antidote to start looking for." Amanda grabbed Sarah's left wrist. "Let's go, honey. Time is wasting."

"I can't let him—"

"He'll be back," Amanda promised Sarah. "He'll get halfway down the trail and come to his senses, you wait and see."

Nolan lowered his gun. "Take a hike, the both of you," he said, and ran over to the unconscious Noel. Sarah and Amanda watched him hoist Noel onto his shoulders and step back. "Once I leave, you two are on your own. You can try to walk out of here, to reach a hospital or whatever you think is right. But if you try to follow me—I'll kill you." And with those words, Nolan turned and staggered away with Noel over his shoulder.

Sarah aimed her gun at his legs, but Amanda shook her head. "Don't," she begged. "Let him go."

"He'll infect—"

"He'll be back," Amanda promised.

"How can you be so sure?" Sarah pleaded, as she kept her gun at the ready.

"Because as screwed up as that guy is—he has a conscience," Amanda sighed. "Come on, Los Angeles, we have to start looking for an antidote—if there is one."

Sarah felt her arms grow weak. Her head hurt as the dizziness seemed to come back. She lowered her gun and watched Nolan vanish around the cabin and out of sight. "My head hurts from trying to figure out the truth, June Bug. Honestly, all I know is that Noel is insane, and Nolan is following right behind her." Sarah looked around. "I don't know how to make heads or tails of this."

"And you thought being a Los Angeles homicide detective was tough work, huh?" Amanda tried to joke, but stopped when she felt a sudden wave of dizziness strike her. "Oh my," she gasped, "dizzy, too."

Sarah steadied Amanda and helped her up onto the front porch and sat her down on a rocking chair. "June Bug, even if Noel did bring extra antidotes with her—what are the chances that we would find them? I'm sure she hid them in a secure location. We don't have time to play hide and seek."

Amanda rubbed her temples. "You know—I've been thinking—how did Noel appear in the kitchen? I mean, she kinda appeared like a puff of smoke, remember?"

"I remember."

Amanda continued to rub her temples. "When Nolan said he watched Noel drag Mrs. Kraus down into a hidden cellar, it occurred to me that maybe that was how she entered the kitchen without being seen or heard. I mean, we had the doors and windows locked up tight. I suppose she could have sneaked in somehow, or had a key, but the kitchen door was still locked and the piles of dishes we'd stacked against it were still in place."

Sarah bit down on her lip. "June Bug, you may be on to something," she said, in an urgent voice. "Sit tight. I'm going to find that hidden cellar."

"I want to come."

"You need to sit right here and stand guard," Sarah ordered Amanda and placed her gun into the hands of her best friend. "Just pull the trigger if he comes back," she said, and ran into the cabin before Amanda could object. But instead of racing into the kitchen, Sarah hurried down into the basement and made her way to the back on nervous legs. And there, to her horror, she saw that Noel had set up some kind of mad scientist experiment. But to her relief—if relief was possible—she saw the remaining virus tubes still sitting in the steel rack on the desk. Sarah quickly grabbed the two tubes and ran upstairs, looked around, and then decided to hide the tubes in a spare bedroom under a loose floorboard. With the tubes secured, she ran into the kitchen and began stomping on the kitchen floor, listening for hollow sounds. The kitchen floor was solid and hard in the middle, but when Sarah walked into the far corner of the kitchen, a location she had not explored the night before, she heard the sound of her foot transfer from a solid thumping noise into a hollow thudding sound.

Sarah quickly dropped down to her knees and began feeling the floor. As far as she could see, she was simply in the broom corner of the kitchen, where rows of hooks held ratty old brooms and an antique-looking metal dustpan. It was certainly no place special. But then her hand felt what seemed like a piece of fishing line, a very short piece in a loop.

"Bingo," Sarah said and with all of her might yanked up on the piece of fishing line as hard as she could. As she did, a piece of climbing rope slithered out from under a floorboard. Sarah quickly grabbed the rope and yanked up on it. To her relief, a loud creak cried out through the kitchen and a hidden trap door that had been set into the kitchen floor with perfect precision and camouflage opened. "Thank you," Sarah whispered.

With no time to waste, Sarah bent down over the dark hole below and peered down into a deep dungeon. She spotted a faint light crawling up from the hole. The light splashed onto a wooden ladder connected to the left wall. Sarah drew in a deep breath, swung her legs down into the hole, found the ladder with her feet, and began to crawl down, one careful step at a time. The ladder moaned and complained under her weight—and for a second, seemed ready to collapse—but it held. "Smells awful down here," Sarah whispered, descending lower and lower down into the earth. Raw earth began to surround her. In her mind, she pictured the kinds of nasty beetles and snakes that might love a damp, dark hole like this one. "Stop it," Sarah begged, and pushed the awful thoughts from her mind. She had no time to waste on thoughts that were not practical or helpful. "There could be an antidote down here."

When Sarah reached the bottom of the ladder, she stepped down onto packed dirt and looked around. A large open room stood before her. To her shock, the room held a table, two chairs, a metal filing cabinet and boxes holding lab equipment. But to her horror, a dead body was resting in the far right corner partially covered over with a brown sheet. "It's like a horror movie down here," she said, thinking immediately about how the coroner would need to be notified; but she ignored that thought as her eyes locked onto a black backpack sitting on the table. "Oh please," Sarah begged as she ran to the table and snatched open the black backpack with shaky hands and began exploring the contents.

"Come on—come on—" she said, pulling out pens, medical books, trail mix, bottled water, clothing—but no antidote. "No, no!" Sarah nearly began to cry. She threw the backpack across the room and then kicked the table. Before she could vent her fury any further, a wave of dizziness attacked her head. This time the dizziness was accompanied by a slight wave of nausea. "No time—" Sarah whispered and grabbed her stomach. She bent forward and began taking in deep breaths. "I have to calm down and think. What would Pete tell me to do?" Sarah closed her eyes and walked her thoughts all the way to Los Angeles, through heavy traffic, clear blue skies, palm trees, tall buildings, and sandy beaches, and wandered into a stuffy office filled with files, Chinese food, and cigar smoke. She spotted her old partner sitting behind his desk smoking a cigar and going over a case file. *"Hey, Pete."*

Pete looked up from the case file and studied Sarah. "You went and got yourself into a mess, didn't you, kiddo?" he asked and took a puff off his cigar. The cigar smoke drifted into Sarah's nose and brought back countless warm memories that nearly made her cry.

"I was bushwhacked, Pete," Sarah explained. "I'm in a real bad spot."

"Well, you gave this case your best shot, but there were too many unknown variables for you to fuss with. Who knew Noel was lying through her teeth?"

"I should have known."

"No cop is perfect, kiddo," Pete pointed out and snatched up a cup of coffee and took a drink. "You found the journal."

"Yeah, but—"

"And by doing so you managed to get the truth from that low-down scumbag," Pete continued.

"Pete, I don't care about Noel or Nolan right now. Amanda and I are infected with a deadly virus—we're dying, and we need help," Sarah begged. "What do I do?"

Pete took another puff from his cigar. "You know what to do. Now think."

"Pete, Noel played me like a fiddle," Sarah confessed in a miserable voice.

"Oh, stop kicking yourself and focus," Pete griped. "Now think back. You already know what you need to do, kiddo. Think about the look Noel gave you when you mentioned the hot springs. You've been thinking about it in the back of your mind this whole time, haven't you? Tell me this—she wasn't standing outside waiting for you for no reason, she was concerned and preparing to go look for you. Why?"

Sarah thought back to the basement. In her mind, she saw herself talking about the hot springs to Noel—and then she saw the strange look flash across Noel's eyes. "Oh my goodness—that look—it was a look of worry. Oh, Pete, that's why I can't find an antidote—the hot springs are the antidote."

"Well, maybe not the only antidote, but I would sure go see if they do something," Pete ordered Sarah. "All I know is that this crazy woman is very deadly and she didn't want you getting in the hot springs. So that's exactly where you should go." Pete puffed on his cigar and looked at a case file. "Now get out of here and let me get back to work, kiddo. I don't have time to babysit a rookie."

Sarah opened her eyes. Pete vanished. "The hot springs," she said, and began coughing. With each cough, droplets of blood began to spray into the air. "Have to—hurry—the virus is maturing." Sarah scrambled up the ladder, ran outside onto the front porch, and found Amanda hunched over the front porch rail vomiting.

"We're—done for," Amanda told Sarah with tear-filled eyes. "There's blood in my vomit."

"We're not dead yet," Sarah promised Amanda. "Gather all the strength you have and come on!" Sarah grabbed Amanda's right arm and raced away toward the hot springs, trying not to trip. The track back to the hot springs almost proved impossible. With each step, Sarah grew weaker and Amanda nearly fainted. They held each other up by sheer force of will. By the time they reached the hot springs, both women only had enough strength left to collapse into the first hot spring. "Amanda," Sarah begged, "keep your head above the water."

Amanda, who was barely conscious, managed to roll her head above the hot waters of the spring, resting it on a smooth rock behind her. "Los Angeles, I love you," she whispered.

"Love you too, June Bug," Sarah replied with all of her heart as the world began to turn dark. For a minute, she thought she'd dropped into an unconscious state, but then her eyes popped open as an excruciating pain began to burn through her body like a raging wildfire. Sarah cried out in pain but managed to keep her body plunged into the hot waters. A few seconds later, Amanda's eyes sprung open and she began to scream in pain. "The water, the temperature is killing the virus!" Sarah yelled, writhing in agony.

"I feel like I'm on fire—burning alive inside," Amanda cried. She began to crawl out of the hot spring, but Sarah pushed her back down.

"Stay under the water," Sarah begged.

"I don't think I can stand it," Amanda cried out in pain. "I'm burning—alive."

"Try," Sarah pleaded with every ounce of energy she had, gripping her friend's arms tightly beneath the water even though she too felt like they were being boiled alive.

"Okay, I'll try," Amanda promised, and began fighting her pain. "Los Angeles, please forgive me for getting you into this mess."

"Misery loves company," Sarah replied, gritting her teeth in pain.

"If we survive, I'm going to buy you the prettiest dress O'Mally has," Amanda promised, and nearly peed herself.

"Deal," Sarah promised, and squeezed her eyes closed, waiting to either burst into flames or die. The pain seemed to come and go in waves, and just when it seemed to abate it would come back in force, as if their blood had circulated and found a new pocket of virus that needed to be destroyed. After an agonizing hour of painful fiery sensation, Sarah felt her body begin to ease off and it seemed the waves of pain stopped altogether. "Hey—I think I'm—done burning it off," she told Amanda in an excited voice. She was still shaky from the heat of the hot springs and the terror of the situation, but she was so grateful to be alive she sent up a silent prayer of thanks.

Amanda looked at Sarah. Relief was in her eyes. "Me,

too," she said, and began to cry. "Do you think the virus is dead?" she asked.

"Yes," Sarah answered her best friend and began to laugh and then cry, all at the same time. "I don't know how, but this hot springs killed the virus." After another twenty minutes or so when they were sure no more fiery pain was going to occur, Sarah took Amanda's hand and pulled her out of the hot springs and hugged her. "We're going to live, June Bug—we're going to live to see another day."

Amanda wrapped her arms around Sarah and cried. "I was so afraid I would never see my hubby or son again. I was trying to be brave." Amanda placed her head down onto Sarah's shoulders and cried until it hurt. They sat down together on a dry log to rest their shaky muscles. When Sarah finished crying, she looked up. "What now?" she asked, looking around at the beautiful wilderness in confusion.

"Now," Sarah said, with an angry voice, "we're going to go catch us two very dangerous bears." Sarah took Amanda's hand and stood up, and they made their way back to the cabin. "We're going to change our clothes and get ready for war," she promised in a determined voice that sent hope into Amanda's heart. It was time to capture a deadly virus.

chapter seven

Sarah was sitting on the front porch sipping a cup of coffee when Nolan came walking back around the cabin holding Noel's arms behind her back. She immediately put down her coffee and picked up her gun. "Hello," she said, in a stern voice. "I assumed you would be miles away by now."

Nolan coughed blood into the air and threw Noel down onto the ground. Noel landed hard, spun around, and kicked her legs at Nolan. "You're dying!" she laughed, in a sick, demented voice. "You're all dying. My virus has matured in your system just like I knew it would."

Before Noel could say another hateful word, Amanda appeared behind Nolan and gently took his arm. Nolan looked at her, surprised to see her looking completely healthy and normal. Amanda let out a soft smile and a wink. "Come with me," she whispered, and pulled Nolan away from the cabin as quickly as she could. Nolan followed without question, too weak to fight. Amanda rushed him to the path that led to the hot springs.

"Where is she taking him?" Noel demanded.

"You'll find out later," Sarah said, and aimed her gun

directly at Noel. "I don't know what kind of sick game you're playing, Noel, but the game has come to an end."

Noel climbed to her legs and brushed the dirt off her knees. "I'm in control, Sarah. I've always been in control. Dr. Kraus could have joined me, but instead, he betrayed me. Nolan, too."

"You lied to me."

"Lies are a matter of perspective. It's all part of the game—allowing people to believe the lies can be very delicious, too," Noel told Sarah. Then she stood very still and studied Sarah's face. As she did, a strange expression—fear and sick foreboding—washed over her face. "You're not exhibiting any symptoms? Why?" she demanded, as anger rushed into her eyes. "You should be. You should both be too weak to move by now."

Sarah stood up, showing off with a straight posture and clear eyes. "I found your antidote," Sarah deliberately lied in order to fish some truth out of Noel.

"Impossible! I buried the antidote in the cellar!" Noel cried out.

"So, you did bring an antidote with you after all," Sarah said, and cautiously stepped down off the front porch. "You're a very disturbed woman. Last night, you had me eating out of your hand."

"I'm just doing what I need to do," Noel snapped. "My task is too important to let a little thing like deceit get in the way."

"Your task is killing millions of people?"

"My task is control," Noel told Sarah, and her voice lowered to a menacing register. "Control is power. All my life I've let men have the authority. I even had two men shoot me in the back and leave me for dead while my so-called husband stood nearby." Noel narrowed her vicious eyes. "My virus is ready. The virus Dr. Kraus created was a threat to me." Noel kept her eyelids low. "He created three different viruses—test viruses, if you will. That's what you found in the basement. Mrs. Kraus hid one of the tubes from me. She assumed by doing so she could blackmail me for more money, or to keep me from reaching my goal, anyway."

Sarah struggled to keep up. Her body was healing from Noel's virus at a rapid rate, but the long stay in the hot springs had drained her muscles and made her feel exhausted to the point of collapse. She couldn't let Noel understand how tired she truly felt. "Mrs. Kraus sprayed your virus because she was injected with an antidote. That's why you shot her."

"I was foolish to trust anyone," Noel told Sarah. "I believed I could trust a fellow woman. A woman who had cared for me for many years. I was wrong." Noel studied Sarah's eyes. "I'll find the missing tube and destroy all three viruses Dr. Kraus created." A sick grin touched Noel's lips. "Dr. Kraus was uncertain of himself. He created three viruses that are worthless against my virus."

"How can you be so sure of that? Have you tested his viruses?" Sarah asked.

"I don't need to," Noel answered, in an arrogant voice. "My mind is far more brilliant than his was. I'm in control, Sarah." Noel kept her eyes on Sarah. "You seem to be... well. I suppose you're not lying, and you did find the antidote I hid in the basement." Noel folded her arms together. "When you mentioned the hot springs, I became—concerned. Of course, your theory about the hot springs was merely theoretical, yet you somehow managed to strike near the truth. My virus, once it matures, can only survive at a certain temperature range within the body. No one can have a fever over 102.2."

"Explain," Sarah told Noel, hoping to gain a deeper understanding of the virus.

"Gladly," Noel replied, in a cavalier tone. "I designed my virus to attack the human immune system, which creates, at a very rapid rate, deadly cancer cells designed to attack the lungs, the heart, the brain, the liver, while at the same time bypassing typical flu-like symptoms such as a sore throat, fever, runny nose. That way there is very little sign of the infection until it is too late."

Sarah soaked in the information. "And the viruses Dr. Kraus created?" she asked.

Noel's eyes grew dark with fury. "Dr. Kraus created three viruses to counteract mine. Well, to counteract the firewalls I created to suppress the flu-like symptoms. His viruses were designed to attack the immune system and specifically activate a fast-acting flu strain that triggers high fevers—well, high enough. Right around 102.2 or higher." Noel gritted her teeth. "The bug I planted, Dr. Kraus located it. He assumed he blinded my operation. He wasn't aware that I had his dear old wife working for me."

"Why did Mrs. Kraus start working for you? Why did she betray her husband?" Sarah asked.

"Mrs. Kraus despised her husband for taking her away from civilization and forcing her to live like a bear in the wild. Mrs. Kraus was a city woman, Sarah. She met her husband on the busy streets of New York while working as an interpreter at the United Nations." Noel smiled in a hideous way. "A woman can discover a lot of secrets while working at the United Nations." She let out a sick laugh. "The United Nations is the largest terror organization in the world, and the silly people of America work their hands to the bone to pay their salaries."

"You mean through taxes? Taxes paid my salary as a cop too, you know."

Noel nodded. "You should be freed from such slavery! Sarah, you may see me as a monster, but you have to understand that my intentions are good. I mean to destroy the men who sit high and proud in this world, in order to allow women to rule in their place." Noel unfolded her arms and motioned around. "Look around, Sarah, look what man is doing to this world. Look how men are suppressing women, creating wars, destroying all of the natural resources, and teaching women and girls that they are dogs."

"My husband teaches love and care," Sarah corrected Noel. "My husband takes care of me and would die for me in the blink of an eye. My husband helps me wash dishes and cooks dinner when I am hard at work. My husband rubs my legs at night and asks me how my day was. My husband brings me flowers and offers me a love I never thought I would find after my first husband divorced me." Sarah shook her head. "One man hurt me—another man healed my broken heart. You can't hate the world for the actions of a few, Noel. Not all men are bad and not all women are good."

"You're just trying to justify—"

"You murdered a woman in cold blood. What does that make you?" Sarah snapped.

"I eliminated a threat," Noel snapped back.

"The so-called criminals inside the United Nations, with their allegedly sick and twisted actions, are only doing the same thing, right? What makes you any different from them? They start wars and kill—you have started a war and you have killed. They want power and control—you want power and control. Noel, you are no different than they are."

"Shut up!" Noel screamed, and grabbed her head. "I'm a woman—proud, brilliant and powerful. I will change everything. I will—"

"You're lost in a fantasy world! And you married Nolan!" Sarah yelled back. "You must not have been as liberated as you hoped."

"I married Nolan because—because—" Noel's mind began to crumble. Sarah was backing her into a corner. "I married Nolan because—"

"Because you fell in love and love felt good, didn't it?" Sarah said. "Love is pure, Noel—sweet to the heart and healing to the soul. You felt a love that covered over the ugly sores infesting your soul!"

"Shut up!" Noel yelled, and charged at Sarah.

Sarah fired a single shot into the ground. "Not another step," she warned Noel. "Now, get down on the ground. You're under arrest."

Noel stopped running and stared at Sarah with deadly eyes. "I'm no fool," she hissed. "I always have a contingency plan." Noel pointed south. "I have already set my virus inside the Anchorage airport. I placed the virus in a heating and air duct. A little bomb is attached to the virus to spread it through the entire system."

"You're lying."

"Am I?" Noel grinned, standing up a little straighter as control returned to her mind. "If I don't dial the bomb's control unit every four hours and speak a code into the device —boom—the bomb goes off and the virus is carried out of the air ducts and sprayed all over the airport."

Sarah felt panic rise in her heart. She knew Noel was speaking the truth. The woman was insane and had no reason to lie—it was far too late in the game to lie. The truth, the complete truth, was now laid out on the table. "You intend to set off that bomb no matter what we do."

"Of course," Noel grinned. "But first I needed to see how my little baby worked. I needed—lab rats, in the form of human beings. Mrs. Kraus informed me that the White Cell was upset with her husband for not spraying Amanda and her husband with the virus he had created. The White Cell, of course, did not know that his virus was meant only to kill mine, which was far more deadly, or that Kraus had been ordered to bring your close friend back here through deceptive means. Well, I saw an opening."

Sarah nearly shot Noel on the spot in a blind rage, but regained her temper, realizing she could ill afford to explain that to the authorities later. Besides, she needed the woman alive. "You're going to deactivate your bomb."

"Or what?" Noel laughed. "Are you going to shoot me,

Sarah?" Noel shook her head. "Sarah, you're not a killer. You're one of those goody-two-shoe cops and foolishly believe you can save the world. In reality, you're just a peon—a nobody, a nothing. Why? Because you think caring about mankind will actually make a difference? You're nothing more than a fool."

"I would rather care for one friend and die a fool, than kill millions and live as a tyrant," Sarah said, throwing her words at Noel as if they were live rounds.

Sarah's words struck Noel in the face. Noel hissed. "You're truly an idiot, then."

"Maybe," Sarah agreed, "but I'm an idiot with a best friend—no, a sister—who would lay down her life for me in a split second. I have a husband who loves me. I have friends who care about me. Maybe I am a fool for caring, but in the end, when I die, I will have caring eyes looking at me. What will you have, Noel? Who will look at you? Nobody except the doctor who will inject deadly chemicals into your veins while you're lying strapped to an execution table."

Noel felt her control leaving her again. "Shut up!"

Sarah realized that Noel feared death—feared the truth—and she understood that using the truth against Noel was the perfect weapon. "Why?" she asked. "Are you afraid of the truth coming out, Noel? Are you afraid that in the end when death comes for you, you'll be all alone?"

"You have no idea what I've been through in my life—no idea! How dare you stand there and judge me? How dare you assume that you know anything about me!"

"Don't give me that," Sarah fired at Noel. "In life there is truth and then there is garbage." Sarah stepped closer to Noel. "The tyrants brainwash people with lies—filthy, ugly, garbage-filled lies. Tyrants manipulate and create social engineering campaigns to brainwash the youth of the world. American kids today can't tell you what the eighth amendment is or who the second president of the United

States was. They couldn't tell you the first thing about the signing of the Declaration of Independence—but they can spew the garbage taught to them through trashy media programs. They know more about the Kardashian's than they know about the war in Iraq." Sarah pointed at Noel. "The battle for truth is being fought all around us, Noel, and the truth will prevail because in the end, lies can only destroy the very foundations of society."

"Nice speech, Sarah, but your words are futile," Noel told Sarah. "My eyes and ears are fully aware of the social engineering campaign being carried out against the youth of the world. I intend to change that. I intend to undo the centuries of oppression and teach women world dominance. Perhaps even force the worst of the men into slavery as they have done to women for so long. I intend to lead the women of the world into a new era, controlling countries, resources, land—"

"You intend on becoming a world dictator? How does that make you any better from these men you hate?" Sarah snapped. "In the end, because you will suppress freedom, you will create a world still full of the same old hate, death, misery and war. The women you assume will obey you and do your bidding will turn against you because, Noel, women aren't slaves to men now, and they certainly don't want to see men enslaved. You have a sick and twisted view of the world if you think women are simply going to leave behind the husbands and families they love so dearly. And this may come as a shock to you, but men love their wives and love their families, too."

"You are so blind," Noel hissed.

Sarah threw her hands in the air and backed off. She had pushed Noel to the edge with the truth and now needed to focus back on the bomb. "If you release your virus in the Anchorage airport, you will kill millions of women."

"An acceptable loss," Noel replied.

"Tell that to the women who are going to die. Will they still accept you as their leader once they find out you killed so many innocent lives to achieve your aims?"

"Power demands servitude," Noel answered.

"You mean you're going to force every woman to serve you whether they choose to or not?" Sarah asked. "Some freedom," she snorted.

Noel stared at Sarah. Sarah was peeling back one layer of truth after the next, forcing her into a deep dark corner, and out of fear she began to kick and claw her way out. "You have one hour before the bomb explodes," she warned Sarah. "Either set me free or I will refuse to dial the code. The death of millions will be on your conscience, not mine."

Sarah stared at Noel and then checked her watch. Assuming Nolan would live if he reached the hot springs in time, still needed more time to wait out the virus dying in his body. Sarah needed to buy time. She needed to make sure Nolan was going to live and that he and Amanda made it back to the lodge. Then, Sarah thought, she was going to have to roll up her sleeves and put two deadly bears down into a deep cellar.

Nolan felt his body begin to burn and struggled to crawl out of the hot spring. Amanda took her foot and kicked him back down. "That's the virus burning out of your system," she said, and aimed Nolan's gun at him. "I'm in no mood to play, you slimy bloke, so sit down and heal."

Nolan stared up at Amanda with weak eyes and then gritted his teeth in pain. He felt like his insides were being doused with gas and lit on fire. "I'm burning alive, the water is too hot."

"You'll live," Amanda replied. "It's not the water. It's the virus dying inside you. Just be grateful that these sweet waters have the power to heal and not kill." Amanda stepped back from the hot spring. "I knew you would come back. I didn't think you would get too far. Not with the virus maturing inside of you." Amanda looked around the wild woods. "Sarah is a brilliant detective and she's taught me a few tricks."

"You can't win," Nolan told Amanda in a pained voice. "Noel—she has a bomb attached to a tube, and the tube is full of her virus. The tube is in an air duct at the Anchorage airport. If we don't set her free, she's going to activate the bomb. My wife—the woman I fell in love with—is dead. I don't know who she is now."

Amanda drew in a deep breath. "Right now, I have to focus on you," she told Nolan. "Even though you're a sewer rat in my view, you are still human. I want you to live long enough to answer to the justice system."

"Oh, I wouldn't count on that," a vicious voice said.

"Huh?" Amanda spun around and saw a man wearing a black assault uniform, like the one Nolan was wearing. The man pointed a gun directly at Amanda. "Oh dear," Amanda whined.

"Drop the gun."

Amanda dropped Nolan's gun and stepped back toward the hot springs. "Who are you?" she asked, staring into a clean-shaven face that appeared intelligent if not charming. The man was far from charming, though. Amanda knew she was staring at a cold-blooded killer who had trained his face to deceive. "You can call me Hank."

"You can call him Wilson Jorge," Nolan said, forcing his body to remain in the hot springs. "This man was sent to your town to be a monitor from the White Cell. He's disguised as a cop."

"You're the new deputy," Amanda gasped.

"I was," Wilson agreed. "The boss man started to get a little concerned when you didn't check in, Nolan. He sent me up here to check on you. I found a tree cut down across the road and followed your signal to this location."

Nolan squeezed his hands together in pain. "I deactivated the chip in my arm—there is no way you—"

"There is always a way," Wilson assured Nolan. "When the boss man realized your signal had been deactivated, he had his people triangulate the last known signal. Then he tapped into security system cameras until he found you. He gave me a call and ordered me to come and find you." Wilson shook his head. "Still in love with the crazy woman, are we?"

"She is my wife," Nolan said, in a voice struggling to hold onto a conscious thought.

"She's a dead woman," Wilson corrected Nolan. "Once we locate her, she will die." Wilson focused on Amanda. "And as for you," he said, and pointed at Amanda. "I have been ordered to let you go free. The boss man is not pleased with how his plans have fallen apart. He has ordered me to offer you a choice—go home and forget about what you've seen and heard, or die. However," Wilson added and looked at Nolan, "I'm a little curious as to just what has happened here."

"Noel had old lady Kraus spray her virus in the main cabin, and she infected me, the woman standing here, and the other woman," Nolan said, through gritted teeth.

The color drained from Wilson's face. He took a few steps back. "You're lying. Our intelligence sources have assured us that Noel does not have a virus."

Amanda tossed a thumb back toward the main cabin. "Noel is at the main cabin. Go see for yourself if you don't believe us."

"Impossible," Wilson demanded. "We have men at the airport monitoring Noel as we speak."

"A decoy you idiot," Nolan said. "She's used a decoy for years. Noel is at the main cabin. Sarah is with her, and the woman is a cop. I don't know what is going on at the cabin.

This woman brought me here to burn the virus Noel infected me without of my body."

"The virus can't survive at a certain high temperature," Amanda explained. "My friend and I were both infected and the hot spring burned the virus out of us."

Wilson stared at Amanda and then looked at Nolan. "We had Noel under constant observation. There is no way she could have escaped. The woman at the cabin—that has to be the decoy," he insisted.

"The woman at the cabin is my wife," Nolan tried to scream as the hot waters continued to burn the virus out of his body. He clenched his jaw in agony and fought to keep his limbs under the water, knowing it was his only chance at survival.

Amanda bit down on her lip. "Nolan, how would Noel activate the bomb to release her virus?" she asked, feeling her mind begin to clear up and get back on track. She felt lousy—hungry and weak—but at least she was wearing a fresh green dress and was alive. Of course, she wanted a cool bath, a hot tea, and custard tart, but those things would have to wait. She had to stop a virus.

"Cell phone," Nolan answered, grimacing.

"This far out?" Amanda asked. "There aren't any cell phone towers around for miles and miles—and Anchorage is far away." Amanda continued to bite her lip. "Could it be that the woman at the airport will activate the bomb and Noel is just bluffing us?"

Nolan raised his eyes and looked up at Amanda. "Noel has a special cell phone that can reach to Anchorage—at least that's what she told me."

Amanda looked at Wilson. "Listen, mister," she said, "I have no doubt in my mind that the sick, twisted little woman will release her virus inside the Anchorage airport. She has an evil mind, let me tell you. But with that said, I don't think she can activate the bomb from this far out. All you have to do is look around and see the truth—we're surrounded by hundreds of miles of open wilderness."

Wilson wasn't interested in debating with Amanda. He had escaped and found a location that would allow him to contact his boss. For the time being, he was standing blind. The only thing that showed he was alive was a little red dot on a monitor screen in some computer room filled with technicians who may or may not do their jobs properly if he disappeared. "I have to contact the boss man," he said, in an urgent voice. "I can't leave you two alone, though. I have to secure this location."

Amanda read Wilson's eyes. The man was preparing to kill her. She knew that quick action was needed so she did the only thing she knew how. She dropped down to her knees and grabbed her belly. "Oh, my belly!" she cried out.

"What's the matter?" Wilson demanded. He ran over to Amanda and grabbed her arm. As she did, Amanda raised her head and coughed all over Wilson's face. He froze. His face drained of all color. Amanda didn't waste any time. She grabbed his arm, pulled him forward, and managed to throw him into the hot springs pool Nolan was sitting in. The man landed head first. He came up splashing and coughing, and didn't see Amanda grab Nolan's gun. Amanda fired a single shot in the air.

"Don' move, you smelly skunk!" Amanda yelled, and looked around. She spotted Wilson's gun lying on the ground and picked it up. "Here is how this is going to work," she explained, "you're going to sit in that hot tub for a solid two hours and let the virus I coughed all over you die. If you get out of the hot tub, you'll—well, you'll die." Amanda hoped Wilson bought her lie and wouldn't realize that a healthy woman couldn't infect him. To her relief, Wilson sat very still and listened, fear and panic washing over his face. "Do you understand me?"

"I understand," Wilson promised. "You've locked me in a cage!"

"Nolan," Amanda ordered, "you must—" Amanda stopped talking when she heard something rustling through the woods toward her location. "Oh my," she said, and without wasting a second, took off running. A few seconds later, the grizzly bear came bursting out of the woods as Amanda watched from a hiding spot in the dense trees.

The bear lumbered grumpily over to the hot springs, spotted two scrumptious meals sitting in the water, and attacked. The men cried out in pain and thrashed around trying to avoid the grizzly's deadly claws, but the space was cramped. Nolan, using all the energy he had, managed to escape. But Wilson Jorge fell victim to the angry bear, whose slashing paw caught his throat and ended his life within seconds. The last thing he remembered thinking was how ironic it was that he would die out in the middle of nowhere at the hands of a wild beast, when he was already infected with a deathly virus. The grizzly bear wasn't worried about a virus at all, however. All the grizzly bear cared about was filling his belly and preparing for a long winter's sleep.

As the grizzly bear focused his attention on Wilson, Amanda made tracks back to the cabin. When she heard someone running behind her, she dared to look over her shoulder and saw Nolan stumbling down the trail, barely able to put one foot in front of the other. "Oh—darn," Amanda said, feeling her conscience attack. She spun around and ran to Nolan. "Put your arm around me, you great big idiot!"

Nolan threw his arm around Amanda and together they managed to reach the main cabin. "Bear—big grizzly bear," Amanda told Sarah, breathing hard. She let go of Nolan and collapsed down onto the bottom step of the front porch. Nolan dropped down onto the ground. "I think he got the other guy—"

"What other guy?" Sarah asked, in an alarmed voice.

"One of them," Amanda said, and pointed at Nolan. "He —the bloke I encountered, was the fake deputy that came to Snow Falls. He was ordered to come up here and check on him." Amanda pointed at Nolan. "I think the bear got him."

"The bear did get him," Nolan confirmed, breathing hard but maintaining consciousness. "There was an awful lot of blood. The boss man will send more people. We have to get out of here."

"You're still sick," Sarah told Nolan. "You weren't in the hot springs long enough." Sarah threw her eyes around and then focused back on Noel. Noel was grinning. "Maybe there is a way," she said.

"Let me go and I'll leave this place," Noel promised Sarah. "I'll let you live. If you refuse," Noel assured Sarah, "millions will die because of you."

"Oh shut up, sister!" Amanda yelled. "You can't activate that bomb of yours from this far out."

"I have a satellite phone that can accomplish the job," Noel snapped at Amanda.

"How did you know about the bomb?" Sarah asked Amanda in an urgent voice.

Amanda took a second to catch her breath. "Nolan told me," she explained. "And then that bloke the bear is munching on ran his mouth and told me his lousy flea circus terror bosses are watching some woman at the Anchorage airport they believe is Noel."

Sarah stared at Noel. "Of course," she said, "distraction is the key."

Noel stopped grinning. "Wilson lied."

"How do you know his name?" Amanda asked.

"It doesn't make any sense," Nolan said, struggling to lean up on one elbow. "Unless Wilson was in on this —somehow?"

"Wilson is in love with me," Noel gritted out at Nolan. "I

used his stupidity against him! I told him to manipulate your boss man until I released the virus." Noel spat at Nolan. "I needed to be certain my virus would act according to design."

"Enough!" Sarah ordered Noel. "We get the idea."

Amanda stood up and walked over to Sarah. "That bear chose the right bloke to eat," she said, in a grateful voice. "Now, the question is, what do we do about them?"

"Noel hid an antidote down in the cellar. I have to go find it." Sarah looked down at Amanda's hand and saw her holding Nolan's gun. "They move—just shoot them, June Bug. No games, honey. Just shoot them."

"I wish you would shoot me," Nolan begged. "My life is over anyway. If you don't kill me, the boss man will. So do me a favor and put me out of my misery."

"Don't tempt me," Amanda warned Nolan. She shook her head and let her eyes soak in the beautiful landscape. "All I wanted to do was buy this land and have my own hot springs resort—or hideaway—or whatever you want to call it. Was that really too much to ask? Blimey, you Americans make living a peaceful life so blasted difficult. I admit that my country has its share of problems, but you Americans take the cake. No offense to you, Los Angeles—you're okay."

"No offense taken," Sarah promised, wiping her hands on the gray work dress she had put on after the hot springs. "I need to get down into the cellar and find the antidote."

"Less than one hour and millions die," Noel warned Sarah. "Let me go—or else!"

Sarah looked into Amanda's eyes. "Honey, this is your call."

Amanda stood, shocked. "But you're the one with all the answers—you're the brilliant detective. I'm simply the silly sidekick."

Sarah took Amanda's hand. "Honey, you're not a silly sidekick. Right now, I need you to tell me what to do. My plan was to lock these two in the cellar and go for help. But this situation is out of my control. All I know to do is find the antidote and save that man's life. After that—what do we do?" Sarah felt desperation grab her heart.

Amanda stared into her friend's eyes and felt a strange peace wash over her. "There is no way that she-monster can detonate her bomb from this far out. Her decoy, honey, she'll be the one to activate the bomb."

"That still means the virus will be set loose to kill millions," Sarah told Amanda, and bowed her head. "Noel—has won. We—no—I, I failed to stop her."

"That's right," Noel laughed. "Even if you hold me here, you still lose—the entire world will lose. I will have my revenge and my victory."

"Oh shut up," Amanda told Noel, and raised Sarah's chin with a loving hand. "Los Angeles, you figured out the hot springs could save us. You didn't fail. Even if the virus is set free, we have a way to kill it—a very painful way—but a way. And hey, wouldn't that bring this place a lot of business?" she tried to joke.

Sarah felt a weak smile touch her lips. "I better go find the antidote and—" Sarah stopped talking and raised her eyes skyward. In the distance, she heard what sounded like a helicopter approaching. She lowered her eyes and looked at Amanda.

All Amanda could say was, "We have company."

Far away, up in the sky, four armed killers, along with a man in his early seventies, waited for the helicopter to deliver them to the battleground.

chapter eight

Sarah grabbed Nolan's right arm and tried to make him stand up. "What's the point?" he asked, and coughed as the virus began to take control of his body again. Nolan's body temperature was lowering and traces of the virus were struggling to reanimate. "Let me die."

"Get up!" Sarah yelled, and pulled Nolan to his feet. "Amanda, get Noel inside!"

Amanda walked over to Noel and used a bandana to tie the woman's hands together behind her back. But before the woman could say a word, Amanda clocked her in the jaw, too, and she fell unconscious to the floor. "I'm not in the mood for games," she said, in an urgent voice, hearing the helicopter growing closer and closer. "Better you go to sleep for a while than risk escape."

Sarah stared at Amanda, then nodded her head. "You would have made a tough street cop."

"I'm a very scared housewife who just wants to see her hubby and son again," Amanda told Sarah and began dragging Noel's unconscious body up the front porch steps. "Blimey, she's heavier than she looks."

Once Amanda had Noel up on the porch, she tried to help

Nolan climb the front porch steps. "I need you to fight," she told Nolan.

Nolan patted his right arm. "I have a chip in me," he explained. "Wherever I run to, the boss man will find me. He's not arriving alone—he'll have armed men who will hunt us all down and kill us." Nolan fought against Sarah's hands. "Let me run off into the woods. I'll go to the hot springs and act as a decoy."

"You're still sick," Sarah told Nolan. "You'll never make it—"

"You go find the antidote," Nolan begged Sarah. "I'll go hide—the boss man will find me no matter where I run. I might be able to hold them off for a while—you can escape."

"You're infected," Sarah said, in a stern voice, hearing the blades of the helicopter growing closer and closer. In another two or three minutes the helicopter would be landing right in front of the main cabin. "I have to give you the antidote."

"I'll—" Nolan struggled to think, but then his eyes rolled up in his head and he collapsed, his face pale and bloodless.

"Get Noel inside. I'll get Nolan!" Sarah yelled at Amanda.

"But the chip in his arm—"

"We'll throw him down into the cellar and find the antidote," Sarah explained. "That's all we can do," she said, in a furious voice, lugging Nolan step by step. "We need to hurry."

Amanda nodded her head, grabbed Noel's arm, and began dragging her into the cabin. "Lay off the donuts, sister," she fussed.

Sarah appeared in the doorway and began dragging Nolan down the long hallway. When she reached the kitchen, she ran to the hidden cellar door, yanked it open, and without wasting any time, simply pushed Nolan's unconscious body down into the hole. Noel followed. "Hurry," Sarah said, and pointed down at the back door.

"Oh," Amanda fretted. She ran to the back door, opened it,

and bolted outside as Sarah slammed the cellar door shut and followed. "Where to?" Amanda asked, hearing the helicopter landing.

Sarah pointed to the woods. "Hurry!"

Amanda grabbed Sarah's hands and darted into the woods. Her frantic mind began to focus on the grizzly bear. "Honey, we have to be careful. There's a hungry bear in these woods."

Sarah ran deeper into the woods as the helicopter finally touched down. As soon as the helicopter touched solid earth, the four armed killers jumped out and stormed up to the cabin. Richard Whitefield followed on slow legs. "Two in the front and two in the back," he yelled, holding what appeared to be a black cell phone. On the screen of the black phone, he studied a red dot that was surrounded by precise landscape. "Our target is inside of this cabin." Richard lowered the phone and looked around. "No one leaves here alive," he yelled. "We're here to clean up an ugly mess and abort a disastrous plan."

As Richard approached the front porch, Sarah tugged Amanda deeper into the woods. "We have to find the four-wheeler Noel arrived on," she explained, running past tall trees and through thick brush. "She told me it was somewhere in the woods."

"If we don't get lost or eaten by a bear, maybe we might have a chance, love," Amanda said, forcing her legs through the untamed, rugged wilderness.

"That hidden trail has to be around here someplace," Sarah explained. "Nolan ran around the cabin with Noel on his shoulder and he returned the same way."

"Whatever you say, love," Amanda replied, keeping pace with Sarah. "All I know is that when we get home, I'm going to sleep for a week."

Sarah slid to a stop behind a tall tree and caught her breath. She threw her eyes to the left and to the right. "I think the hot springs are that way," she said, and pointed to her left.

"Then we go this way," Amanda said, and pointed to her right. "That grizzly bear is at the hot springs." Amanda rolled her eyes. "Noel and her stories—oh, the grizzly bear is harmless—it's so lovely to spend time with people who understand me—my foot."

"Noel was deceiving us," Sarah told Amanda. "She spoke with a false tongue all night. She sure fooled me. But," Sarah sighed, "she was shot and left for dead. A part of me still wants to pity her. I know she's mentally insane, but—"

Amanda reached out and grabbed Sarah's face. "Love, that woman is a cold-blooded killer. Snap out of it."

Sarah stared into Amanda's eyes. "She's broken, June Bug. Somewhere in her life, long ago, someone broke that woman and turned her into the monster she is."

"Yeah, and children are dying all over this world from starvation, love, and you don't see them going around wanting to kill millions of people," Amanda pointed out. "Noel may have endured some hard times in her past—hurtful times—but a person has to grow up, pull up their pants, and get on with their life. Noel chose the path she walked—she chose to make her virus—she chose to become the monster she is. If she needs a mental hospital, that's beside the point," Amanda looked around. "There are plenty of mentally ill people in the world, some even worse than her, and they don't all go around infecting innocent people and manipulating others."

Sarah reached out and hugged her best friend. "Thanks, June Bug, my tired mind needed to hear that truth. I know feeling sorry for Noel isn't healthy. I need to continue to see that woman for what she is."

"Dead," Amanda said, and pointed back toward the cabin. "We left her for dead—and good riddance."

"We didn't leave her for dead," Sarah assured Amanda. "Remember, the cabin is still infected with the virus."

"Huh?" Amanda said, and then her eyes grew wide. "Why you little—" she grinned from ear to ear. "You led the wolves straight into a trap."

"When Noel regains consciousness, her brain will start working. She'll realize what I did and use it to her advantage." Sarah kept her eyes on the move. "We couldn't stay back there and fight an army, and there's no way to decontaminate the cabin. All I knew to do was draw in the wolves and make a run for it. Our goal now is to find a phone and call the authorities in Anchorage. And who knows, maybe—just maybe—we'll be able to trap Noel before she escapes."

"How?" Amanda asked.

"Close down the Alaska airspace—shut down the borders —something, anything?" Sarah suggested. She looked back at the cabin. "I left Noel and Nolan with their own war to fight. My focus now is the airport. Let's move."

"Love?" Amanda hesitated.

"Yes?"

"I know the hot springs killed off the virus—but we ran back into the cabin. Could it be we're contaminated again?"

Sarah let out a gentle smile. "I was worried about that but while you were away with Nolan at the hot springs, I tricked Noel into confessing that the virus can't infect a person twice. Otherwise she wouldn't be able to use an antidote to keep people safe, right? I believe she was telling the truth."

"She told us so many lies—how do we know what to believe?" Amanda worried.

Sarah kept her smile. She reached out and touched Amanda's shoulder. "I read her eyes, June Bug. Noel wasn't lying when she told me the virus can't infect a person a second time."

Amanda found comfort in Sarah's voice. "When we get home, I want a hundred blood tests done."

"You bet," Sarah agreed, and pointed to her right. "We need to hurry and—" Sarah stopped. She looked to her left and listened. In the distance, she heard what sounded like a large creature running through the woods. "The bear?" she whispered.

Amanda's eyes grew wide. "Yes," she whispered back.

"We can't outrun a bear in these woods—and if I fire at it, I'll give away our location," Sarah whispered.

"What do we do?"

"Back to the cabins, hurry!" Sarah grabbed Amanda's arm and ran back to the small cabins. She spotted two men walking around the main cabin, waited until the two men vanished out of sight, and dashed into the last cabin—the cabin Nolan had been hiding in. As soon as she closed the front door, the grizzly burst out of the woods, looked around, and lumbered toward the main cabin, its paws shaking the earth. Seconds later, gunfire erupted. "They're shooting at the bear," Sarah told Amanda. "Now is our chance." Once again Sarah eased Amanda back into the woods and took off running. Back at the main cabin, the grizzly bear limped off into the woods, wounded but not dead.

"That bear," Amanda fussed under her breath. "First it eats our food, then tries to eat us—some thanks."

Sarah kept dragging Amanda through the woods, seeking the back paths and trails. When they finally found one that looked like it led the correct direction, they ran for what seemed like forever. And then, to Sarah's relief, they burst out into a small clearing. A four-wheeler covered with a camouflage tarp was resting in the clearing. "Thank you," Sarah prayed, and nearly burst into tears. She let go of Amanda, yanked the tarp off the four-wheeler, and smiled. "We're going to be okay, June Bug."

"You bet we are," Amanda said, and pointed to what

appeared to be a wider trail leading downhill. "I think that is our road out of here."

"Let's not waste any time finding out." Sarah jumped onto the four-wheeler and examined the controls. "Not much different than my snowmobile," she said, and managed to bring the four-wheeler to life. "Jump on, June Bug!"

Amanda ran to the four-wheeler, climbed on the seat, wrapped her arms around Sarah's waist and yelled, "Gun it, love!"

Sarah put the four-wheeler into first gear and eased forward at a slow pace. "Let me get used to the gears," she told Amanda, and felt her heart leap with joy. "We're going home."

Amanda placed her head down on Sarah's shoulders and closed her eyes. "Home," she whispered as Sarah began maneuvering the four-wheeler down a rough trail. An hour later, the trail ended on the rugged road leading up to the hot springs. "Well—I'll be," Amanda gasped. "There's the lake. We're not very far from the resort."

Sarah aimed the four-wheeler downhill and took off. "Let's put some distance between us and the bad guys," she said, and looked skyward. "I haven't heard the helicopter, and there's no telling what's happening back at the cabin. I for one, don't want to find out."

"Me neither," Amanda said, and hugged Sarah. "Gun it, love." This time Sarah opened the throttle on the four-wheeler and raced down the rough road at a dangerous speed. Amanda clung on for dear life. When the four-wheeler reached the end of the road and peeled out onto asphalt, Amanda let out a wild yell.

"We did it, June Bug!" Sarah yelled back.

"You found the four-wheeler, love," Amanda laughed, and patted Sarah on her shoulder. "Now, get us to a phone and find me a custard tart and a hot tea."

Sarah laughed and raced the four-wheeler down a long,

remote back road at high speeds. An hour later, she reached the old gas station she had stopped at with Amanda to fill up her jeep. She parked the four-wheeler and leapt out of the seat, and ran to an outside pay phone and called Conrad. He answered on the first ring. "Conrad, it's me, I—"

"I'm sorry," Conrad said, sitting in his office. "We shouldn't have argued. It was all my fault."

Conrad's voice made Sarah break down and start crying. "No, it was all my fault," she promised. But her tears were loud and panicked, far too loud to match the minor disagreement they had had a few days earlier.

"Sarah, what's wrong? Is everything okay?" Conrad asked. He jumped to his feet. "Talk to me. What's happening?"

"Conrad, call the Anchorage police. There's a bomb—well, a virus connected to a bomb, and it's hidden in the Anchorage airport in some air duct. I don't know where, but I do know it's deadly."

"Where are you?" Conrad demanded. "I'm coming to get you."

"I'm at an old gas station on the Snow Ridge Trail Road that branches off of Route 17. Amanda is with me—we're fine," Sarah promised, and wiped at her tears. "Conrad, please, you have to tell them to evacuate the airport." Sarah drew in a deep breath and went into more detail. She explained to Conrad all about Noel. "You have to locate any woman that matches her description."

"I will," Conrad assured his wife, "but I'll let the authorities in Anchorage handle that. I'm coming to get you, Sarah, and I'm never letting you out of my sight again. And that goes for Amanda, too. You girls hang tight. I'll be to you in a couple of hours."

"I—love you," Sarah told Conrad as fresh tears spilled from her eyes. "This entire time all I kept thinking about was you—about us sitting in our kitchen together, drinking coffee, and talking," Sarah wiped at her tears. "When I get home, I'm never leaving your sight again."

"Me, neither," Amanda added, and wiped Sarah's tears away.

"I'm on my way," Conrad promised, and ended the call. He wasn't interested in talking on the phone. He wanted Sarah in his arms as soon as possible.

Sarah handed Amanda the phone. "You better call your hubby."

Amanda winced. "My hubby is going to chew my ear off," she fretted.

"Good," Sarah smiled, and wiped the rest of her tears away. "While your hubby is chewing your ears off, I'll go inside and get us some water and a candy bar apiece. I'm starving."

"Me, too," Amanda said, and let out a tired laugh. "I like caramel candy bars," she told Sarah and then called her husband and winced, waiting to be chewed out from top to bottom. At least, she thought, watching Sarah walking into the old gas station, the air was fresh, cool, and scented with an early snow. The snow would make life better. "Hello—yes, this is your wife, and well, there's been a little problem," Amanda spoke into the phone and then burst out crying. So what if her hubby was going to chew her out? She loved him and she was alive to enjoy their marriage; that's all that mattered now. Sure, she was a strong woman—a fighter—but she knew it took an even stronger woman to love a good man.

Amanda rubbed her arm. "That Dr. Green should be shot," she fussed, and plopped down at the kitchen table resting inside of Sarah's cabin. "This is the fourth time he's drawn blood and every time he jabs me like I'm a raw piece of meat."

Sarah smiled and poured Amanda a cup of coffee. "Maybe it's your dress," she teased.

"My dress?" Amanda asked. She lowered her eyes and looked down at a lovely pink dress covered with a white silk blouse. "I think I look rather dazzling, thank you."

"I was only kidding, June Bug," Sarah laughed and walked Amanda's coffee over to the kitchen table and sat down. "Oh, it's good to be home. After spending a month in Anchorage being examined by every doctor in the world, it's sure good to be home."

"I'm not so sure, with Dr. Happy Needle in town. I can't believe we have to give blood once a week for an entire year," Amanda complained. She glanced at the blue and white dress Sarah was wearing and smiled. It was a relief to see her dearest friend no longer wearing a hospital gown. "You always look so pretty in that dress."

"I wanted to feel pretty today," Sarah explained. "After what we went through—nearly dying—it feels nice to wear a pretty dress and enjoy life again." Sarah took a sip of coffee and nodded at the kitchen window. "It won't be long before we'll be dragging our winter coats out of the closet."

"Oh, I suppose that will be fine," Amanda replied. She picked up her coffee, looked at the kitchen window and then looked at Mittens asleep in the corner. "I love the snow, Los Angeles. I love everything about the snow," she explained, and took a sip of coffee. "The first snowfall is always so clean —so romantic. And now that my dear hubby is home and working on my—our—new dress shop with your husband—life is very sweet again. When the snow arrives it just makes life that much sweeter."

"Bitter winds, freezing snow, slippery roads," Sarah pointed out.

"Warm fireplaces, hot coffee, snowm—" Amanda stopped. "Oh, sorry, love. I didn't mean to—"

"It's okay, June Bug," Sarah assured her best friend. "I

know what you mean." Sarah glanced at the back door. "I still see that awful snowman in my dreams—wearing that awful leather jacket and chewing on a peppermint candy cane. That snowman represents all the evils that live inside of people."

"Love, we're home now. Safe and sound. We have to let all the awful nightmares fade away and focus on—well, custard tarts and hot tea," Amanda said, hoping to bring some humor into the kitchen. Before she could say another word, Mittens raised her head and began growling. Sarah quickly eased her hand down to her ankle and began going for her gun. "Love?" Amanda asked, becoming frightened. She pointed at the pantry door, where Mittens had her eyes trained with urgent alarm.

"Don't move," Noel's voice slithered into the kitchen.

Sarah turned in her chair and saw the pantry door swing open. Noel appeared. "Hello, my friends," she hissed, and aimed a gun at Sarah. "Drop your gun."

Sarah stared at Noel and did as she was ordered. "What are you doing here?"

"Do you always creep around in pantries?" Amanda asked. "Nice outfit, by the way. Black is really your color."

"Shut up," Noel hissed. Her dress was tattered, as if she had been on the run for a long while. She stepped out of the pantry and looked around. "You're all alone," she grinned. "And now, you will die."

"Why aren't you dead?" Sarah asked.

"You left me for dead, didn't you?" Noel asked Sarah. "But as you can see, I'm alive—alive and very angry. Because of you, my plan was destroyed. The police located my virus. But not to worry, I still have a tube of my virus left—hidden in a very safe place. After I kill you, I will carry out my plan—in time."

"Where's Nolan?" Sarah asked. "What happened after we escaped?"

Noel narrowed her deadly eyes. "The boss man, as Nolan

called him, found us in the cellar. But I was prepared. I sprayed him and his men with my virus and managed to escape. It's amazing how being infected with a virus can cripple a man. Whitefield and his men turned into the cowards they are." As she spoke, her eyes darted around as if dissatisfied with something.

"No, it wasn't that simple, was it," Sarah objected, reading Noel's eyes. "Where is Nolan?"

Noel gritted her teeth. "Very well," she hissed, and spoke the truth. "There was a hidden door in the cellar that leads away from the cabin. Nolan, in an attempt to find—absolution—held off Whitfield and his men while I escaped."

"Nolan loved you," Sarah told Noel.

"Nolan is dead," Noel snapped in a heartless voice. "He did allow me time to escape and for that, I suppose I should be grateful. But I'm not here to talk about Nolan. I'm here to finish some very important business. You two ladies caused me a great deal of trouble, and now you're going to suffer the consequences." Noel kicked the pantry door shut behind her. "I'm going to kill you both, then infect your entire town with my virus."

"You're ill," Sarah told Noel, in a sad voice. "You have no soul—no conscience. I once felt very sorry for you, but my friend here helped me realize the truth."

"You're a sick, twisted cookie, sister," Amanda told Noel and took a sip of her coffee. "If you're going to kill us, then do it and stop with all the drama. But let me finish my coffee, okay?" she said, and glanced at Mittens, who had stopped growling, and was now looking toward the living room. Sarah noticed Mittens looking toward the living room, too, which meant only one thing.

"Where is the virus?" Sarah asked Noel. "There's no harm in telling us if you're going to kill us anyway, right?"

Noel studied Sarah's face. "You're not as smart as you appear, Sarah. I know your games."

"What games?" Sarah asked. "You're the one holding the gun. What games can I possibly be playing?" Sarah shook her head and sipped her coffee. "Just kill us already. We're not going to cower down in fear. That's what you want, isn't it? You want us to beg for our lives, right?"

Noel glared at Sarah with furious eyes. "You'll die in fear," she promised Sarah.

"Why don't you just tell me where you hid the virus first?" Sarah asked. "Or are you afraid I'll defeat you again and find your virus? That must be it," Sarah said, deliberately pushing Noel to the edge.

"My virus is hidden—"

"Oh, shut up," Amanda fussed, "just shoot us already. Who cares where you hid the dumb old virus. We figured out how to kill it anyway, so there." Amanda stuck her tongue out at Noel.

Noel grew furious. She glared at Sarah with deadly eyes. "My virus is right here in Snow Falls, Sarah. I am going to release it—but perhaps instead of killing you, I'll make you watch everyone die, instead." Noel's eyes grew darker. "Mr. Whitfield is infected, and he doesn't even know it. He's going to contaminate everyone inside the United Nations building. I won him over, and now, Sarah, I'm going to win you over, too."

Sarah kept calm. "Not likely. Where is the virus, Noel? Where did you hide it?"

"Who cares," Amanda told Sarah, understanding the game. She had to play the role of the bad cop. "This sour tart isn't worth our time. Just let her shoot us and get it over with. I'm tired of hearing her blather way."

"Your words are unpleasant," Noel hissed at Amanda. "And I haven't forgotten that you hit me."

"Oh, shut up," Amanda snapped, and went back to her coffee, hoping Noel wouldn't shoot her.

"Where's your virus, Noel?" Sarah asked again. "Are you

afraid of me? Is that why you won't tell? Because you're afraid I'll over-power you. Again?"

"I'm not afraid of you, Sarah," Noel assured Sarah.

"Then tell me where you hid your virus and prove it. After all, I'm a dead woman. What can I do?"

Noel continued to study Sarah's eyes. She didn't like being called a coward—and she despised being challenged. Her authority was on the line and she had to silence the arrogance of her opposition. "My virus is hidden in a cabin."

"Where?"

"214 Pine Snow Lane," Noel confessed, then pointed a hard finger at Sarah. "Now, Sarah, let's see you try and get my virus from me. Do you think you can?" Noel lowered her finger. "Do you think you can really defeat me, Sarah? I can see in your eyes that you honestly believe you can win the war. So go ahead and try."

"I can't win this war against you, Noel," Sarah replied, her voice sad. "You are mentally ill and need help. But, you're beyond any help that can be offered. The only help for you is —" Sarah stopped talking and looked toward the living room. "Now, honey!" she yelled.

Before Noel could react, a single bullet struck her gun hand. She let out a loud cry, grabbed her hand, and dropped down to her knees. Conrad ran into the kitchen, kicked Noel's gun away from her, slammed the woman down onto her stomach and slapped handcuffs onto her wrists. "I forgot my hammer," he told Sarah, with a grin and a shrug. "I can't build shelves at the dress shop without my hammer."

"Perfect timing, honey," Sarah smiled, and let out a sigh of relief. "Remind me to bronze your hammer."

"How?" Noel cried. "How is this possible?"

Sarah stood up, walked over to Noel, and bent down. "Love," Sarah whispered. "Love will always defeat hate, Noel. Love will never fail. It's true that this world is full of evil and hate, and sometimes evil harms love, but as long as there are people who continue to care and love, hate will never win." Sarah leaned closer to Noel. "Nolan loved you. He gave up his life to protect you. He loved you."

"Shut up!" Noel screamed, as blood poured from her wounded hand. "Shut up—I am powerful. I don't need love, I would never let a man like this control me—"

"I don't control my wife," Conrad told Noel, wrapping her bloody hand in an old kitchen rag. "I love and respect my wife. I would die for her, any given second."

"And I don't control my husband," Sarah continued. "I love and respect him and would die for him at any given second, too." Sarah leaned up and took Conrad's hand. "Noel, I don't know what darkness harmed and destroyed your heart in the past—and I'm truly sorry for whatever happened to you." Sarah shook her head. "But in this life, those who continue to love will never let the darkness win."

"You chose your path, sister," Amanda told Noel, "and now you're going to suffer for it." Amanda stood up, kissed Sarah and Conrad and said, "I think I'm going to go help my hubby build a few dress shelves."

"I'll get you," Noel promised Amanda, struggling on the floor. "No prison in the world can hold me. I'll come for you."

"I'll be waiting," Amanda promised Noel, and began to leave. Then she paused, walked over to Noel, and lifted the woman's face up to hers. "Why?" she asked. "Why do you hate so much?"

"Because I was hated," Noel spat at Amanda. "My parents hated me, I became what they wanted to see—a monster—trying to earn their love. I failed. But it was Kraus who hurt me the most. He never, never held me or told me that he loved me." A single tear dropped from Noel's eye. "I learned that absolute power is the only love I needed."

Amanda wiped Noel's tear away with a gentle hand that shocked everyone. "I'm sorry that you'll never understand love and forgiveness," she whispered, and stood up. "Los

Angeles, I'll be by for coffee later on, after you've cleaned up this mess."

"Coffee will be waiting," Sarah promised, and saw Amanda out. As soon as Amanda was gone, Conrad called the station and ordered two men out to the cabin and then called Anchorage. "I need someone to come and get that virus," he told Sarah.

Sarah nodded and decided to tend to Noel's hand. "Why are you showing me kindness?" Noel demanded, as her hand was washed with disinfectant. "I came here to kill you—to kill everyone in this town."

"It's like my friend said," Sarah told Noel, dabbing her hand with a clean cloth. "It's all about forgiveness. Maybe someday you'll learn what that word means."

Noel rolled over onto her back and stared up at Sarah. "If I ever get the chance—and I will someday—I'm going to return and kill all of you."

"Maybe so," Sarah said, "but it won't be today." Sarah stood up. "On this day, Noel, I forgive you for hating me."

"Fool," Noel hissed. "You are weak."

"Maybe you see it that way," Sarah agreed, and walked over to Conrad and rested her head on his shoulder as he made a call to Anchorage. "And maybe you don't know what strength really looks like. I have someone to keep me strong."

Conrad turned and looked at Sarah and smiled. "Ditto," he said, and kissed Sarah's cheek. "How about dinner at the diner tonight? I could go for a cheeseburger and some fries."

"How about baked chicken and some vegetables?" Sarah smiled.

"Deal," Conrad agreed, and made his call.

Later, after Noel was safely tucked inside a secured jail cell, Conrad and Sarah met Amanda and her husband at the diner for a lovely dinner where they all tried to forget the troubles that Noel had brought to their town. After dinner, Conrad drove Sarah home, made a fresh pot of coffee, and began baking a cake while she rested her feet on an easy chair. "How are you feeling?" he asked Sarah when she got up.

"Fine," Sarah promised, as she hooked a pink leash to Mittens. "I need to take Mittens for a walk."

"I can come—"

"You work on your cake," Sarah smiled. "You're becoming quite the baker. Also," Sarah added, walking Mittens to the back door, "the baked chicken at the diner we had didn't really fill me up. A slice of cake and some hot coffee will really hit the spot."

Conrad leaned against the kitchen counter and looked at Sarah with loving eyes. "You sure are beautiful."

Sarah felt her cheeks turn pink. Even though Conrad was her husband, every compliment he gave her seemed to make her blush. "I love you, too," she smiled. "And speaking of love, maybe we can hike up to our cabin tomorrow and have a picnic? You know how much I love our picnics."

"Supposed to rain all day tomorrow," Conrad explained. He walked over to Sarah and softly kissed her. "But we can spend the entire day inside playing your favorite board games, eating cake and drinking coffee. We can even invite Amanda over."

Sarah considered Conrad's offer. "Well, if we must," she laughed, and kissed Conrad. "I better go walk Mittens before she bursts." Sarah hurried outside into a late evening wind and walked Mittens toward the front road. Before she reached the front road, she paused and listened to the wind playing in the trees. In her mind, she saw the hot springs and all she had faced there, and then she saw a hideous snowman grinning at her from the shadows. "You're still around," she whispered, "but I'm not going to run from you, because I have love—and love will always win." Sarah moved toward the front road with Mittens trotting at her side.

She took a relaxing walk along the chilly and scenic rural

road as the world continued to turn and monsters continued to roam. But for the time being—at least in Snow Falls, Alaska —one deadly monster was locked safely away. At least for a while. Sarah wasn't sure what the future held for a person like Noel, who could not even fathom the kind of love that Sarah held so close to her heart. Sarah only hoped that whatever the future held for the woman, it no longer involved her and her town.

more from wendy

Alaska Cozy Mystery Series

Maple Hills Cozy Series

Sweeetfern Harbor Cozy Series

Sweet Peach Cozy Series

Sweet Shop Cozy Series

Twin Berry Bakery Series

about wendy meadows

Wendy Meadows is a USA Today bestselling author whose stories showcase women sleuths. To date, she has published dozens of books, which include her popular Sweetfern Harbor series, Sweet Peach Bakery series, and Alaska Cozy series, to name a few. She lives in the "Granite State" with her husband, two sons, two mini pigs and a lovable Labradoodle.

Join Wendy's newsletter to stay up-to-date with new releases. As a subscriber, you'll also get BLACKVINE MANOR, the complete series, for FREE!

Join Wendy's Newsletter Here

wendymeadows.com/cozy

Made in the USA
Middletown, DE
30 July 2024

58167202R00086